SHORT STORIES

H A Howe

Copyright © 2014 H A Howe

The moral right of the author has been asserted.

Apart from any fair dealing for the purposes of research or private study, or criticism or review, as permitted under the Copyright, Designs and Patents Act 1988, this publication may only be reproduced, stored or transmitted, in any form or by any means, with the prior permission in writing of the publishers, or in the case of reprographic reproduction in accordance with the terms of licences issued by the Copyright Licensing Agency. Enquiries concerning reproduction outside those terms should be sent to the publishers.

Short Stories by H A Howe is a work of fiction, any resemblance between characters and actual persons, living or dead, is coincidental.

Victory Entertainment Ltd

52, Lancaster Rd

London N4 4PR

victoryentertainment@btconnect.com

ISBN 978 0992906 900

British Library Cataloguing in Publication Data.
A catalogue record for this book is available from the British Library.

Typeset by Troubador Publishing Ltd, Leicester, UK

Let our lives be open books for all to study.

Mahatma Gandhi

CONTENTS

1.	For Love's Sake	1
2.	Just Popping Out	35
3.	Adult Education	39
4.	From Love To Hate – In Ten Seconds	81
5.	A Good Deal	85
6.	Just In Case …	97

FOR LOVE'S SAKE

When he heard the familiar sound of his parents arguing, Charlie temporarily abandoned his intention to get a glass of milk and instead sat down on the top stair, listening, waiting until all was quiet again before venturing downstairs and pretending that he hadn't heard anything. These disagreements were usually about money and Charlie had become so immune to them that more often than not he listened without hearing any of it. He simply daydreamed to the steady hissing noise that was coming from below, sometimes in a muffled tenor, 'You are what you are, not what you want to be', then again a smooth mezzo soprano, 'You once told me I could be anything I wanted to be', until nothing registered except high/low, high/low.

Matt and Sally seemed to disagree on everything these days and they ended up arguing every time they were in the same room together, unless Charlie was present, in which case Sally would hold her tongue and play 'happy family'. She had sat through dinner, smiling and nodding at Matt pontificating about what an important man he was and how, in his former job, the whole company relied on him, 'You see Charlie, that's why your dad was paid a top salary', he had pompously announced, accompanied by a self-satisfied wink in Charlie's direction. For Charlie's sake, Sally was willing to endure Matt's self-aggrandisement because she felt it was important that a son should look up to his father. She did however, store it all up for later, once Charlie had gone to his room. 'So, Mister Bigshot, it's Charlie's school trip at the end of the month and we haven't paid yet'. The subject of money alone was sure to create an argument, the way she brought it up didn't help. Matt hated sarcasm because he himself had never quite mastered it, 'Why doesn't it sink in', he basically spat at her furiously, 'We can't afford it, full stop ... unless, of course, you bloody well go and earn some money quickly!' 'But surely someone as important as you are ...', she started to reply in a honey voice, knowing full well that it would make things worse. But when she saw Matt's half raised hand accompanied by a trembling, 'I swear to God, Sally', she decided to change course. Not that she was scared of Matt in the slightest, it was just that Charlie's school trip was her priority right now. 'Ok Matt', she said in a pleading, matter of fact tone, 'Let's not make this about us. Charlie should be our only consideration here and ...' Matt, unable to share her sentiment, interrupted angrily, 'It's the money, for fuck's sake Sally, we have to consider, not Charlie. We don't have £ 200 to spare! I don't know what the fuck's wrong with you!' Sally was very much aware that money was running out fast but she also knew that they could still afford to pay for their son's school trip as long as they were prepared to cut down on other expenses. Unlike Matt, she was willing to sacrifice anything, financially or otherwise, to see her son happy. And so she chose to ignore Matt's objection and to suppress her own anger, 'He is so looking forward to it. All his pals are going'. But Matt wasn't going to have any of it. 'I don't care', he shouted. He has to get over it ... and so will you! Don't you think it's time to tell him the truth?'

'No, I don't', she shouted. 'He is so young, we can't burden him with our problems. He is the only positive thing in my life right now and I need him to be happy.' Without another word, although his whole body was shaking with anger, Matt took out his chequebook and, remaining standing, wrote out a cheque for £200. He then looked at his wife and declared in a vibrating voice, 'And that's it, Sally ... do it your way, but without me ... I can't take this anymore ... I just can't.' Then, his hand already on the door knob, he added whilst pointing vigorously upstairs, 'I will not spend another penny indulging him!'

Charlie heard the front door open and shut and by the silence that followed he knew it would be alright to get his milk now. What Charlie didn't know was that he would never see his father again.

* * *

When his father still hadn't returned after a couple of days, Charlie eventually decided to ask his mother about it. 'He is away on business, darling', came the pathetic lie which, as always, he pretended to believe. 'Will he be away long?' he asked whilst thinking, 'For somebody who is unemployed, he has rather a lot of business trips'. Charlie was ten years old but had been aware of his parents' deteriorating relationship and their financial fiasco for the past two years, during which time he had become accustomed to the situation, not least due to the heated arguments which had become more frequent lately. But he would never forget the first time he realised that his parents were in financial difficulties. He was so worried when, two years ago, he heard his father say they had fallen behind with mortgage payments and were now forced to sell their house to pay off the debts, and that they had to move somewhere a lot smaller and he wasn't even sure if they could afford anything at all. At the time, Charlie didn't know anything about mortgages and debts, even now, whilst the terms are familiar, he still doesn't understand their concept but what he did grasp then, aged eight, was that he would be losing his home and that thought terrified and haunted him for several days. Unable to sleep without being woken by the sheer terror of nightmares which had him sleeping on park benches surrounded by hungry wolves or in deserted cemeteries fighting off vampires, he finally decided to approach his mother. She just laughed and told him he'd got it all wrong, his father had been talking about one of his colleagues. She assured him that they were as well off as ever and were even planning an exotic holiday in the summer. Whether she did it to protect him because she realised how worried he was or whether her reaction was triggered to save herself the embarrassment did not matter to him at the time. Deep down, had he allowed himself to think realistically, he would have known even then at his tender age that she was lying. But he was not ready to cope with the truth and gratefully accepted her stories. Over time, he carried on pretending to believe her lies but not so much anymore because he didn't want to face the truth, no, it was more to please her because he had noticed how happy it made her to think that he was oblivious to what was really going on. And so he let her think that he believed that his father had to spend at least a year abroad to set up a branch for the company he worked for, and that it didn't make any sense to live in such a big house whilst there were just the two of them, but that the moment his father returned they would move back into a bigger house again. It has to be said, Sally tried very hard to be convincing and never just offered him a blunt statement. She would engage him in long conversations, encourage him to think he was part of the decision making – whether it was better to sell their house or let it and when the best time would be to visit his dad abroad. She had of course, as little say in the matter as he did but the pretence of it seemed to cheer her up, as did the bottle of wine that usually accompanied these discussions.

* * *

After a while, Charlie's father was not mentioned anymore and Charlie and Sally carried on, in their little one bedroom flat, to lie to each other in the firm belief that they were helping the other one by doing so. But Sally did not notice that, as Charlie grew into a teenager, it became increasingly more difficult for him to keep up the charade and to accept their situation without questioning the banality of hiding from the dreary facts of their abysmal life.

Sally adored Charlie. To see him happy was her only goal in life, and she was prepared to do anything to achieve it. She never realised that Charlie's display of happiness was a façade and reflected quite the opposite to how he really felt. When he was fourteen, puberty was intensifying the emotional impact his miserable life had on him. At home he pretended that he was happy, at school he pretended to have a normal home life. When other kids talked about the delicious dinners they had, he was too embarrassed to admit that very often he went to sleep on a few slices of bread and butter because his mother had been too drunk to cook. And when she did prepare dinner, which happened occasionally, her culinary efforts were limited. Even when Charlie was little and long before they had money problems, their weekend lunches were often what Sally called healthy and sophisticated and Charlie's friends referred to as weird and foreign, and consisted of Parma ham or prosciutto, gravadlax, goats' or feta cheese, olives, grilled asparagus and artichokes. Food Charlie had grown up with but which was unfamiliar to most of his friends who used to be shocked when they turned up for Sunday lunch and found there was no roast to be carved. But that was a long time ago, he hadn't had anybody round in years. The last time he had a friend home was about three years ago when Chris turned up unexpectedly. And had Charlie not been in the bathroom when the door bell rang, he would have prevented that visit too. Alas, by the time he ran out into the hall, his mother, in her short, see-through nightie, her dishevelled hair and make-up smeared face leaving no doubt as to her condition, was already forcing Chris over the threshold. Charlie could have died of shame. Chris on the other hand, had no problem in staring at all that was on display and Charlie thanked God that his mother had been too drunk the night before to take off her knickers. It took weeks before the sleazy remarks at school stopped. Well, temporarily at least, until school sport's day, when Sally provided them with more ammunition.

Charlie had begged his mother not to have a drink beforehand or whilst there, figuring that her short, tight denim skirt and even tighter fitting blue and white striped top were enough to start tongues wagging. So when his form teacher offered her a glass of wine, Charlie immediately declined on her behalf saying his mother couldn't drink alcohol. Sally of course was not going to let the opportunity pass and chirped, 'It's alright, darling, I can have a little'. Charlie's lie that she shouldn't be drinking whilst taking antibiotics was a last desperate attempt which was being ignored by his mother as well as his form teacher and could not stop the inevitable. For Sally, as with many shy people, alcohol made her chatty but, like most alcoholics, Sally never recognised the boundaries between being sociable and being unacceptably drunk. A short while later, Charlie almost succeeded in dragging his mother away from the hospitality stand where, deserted by his form teacher, she was swaying back and forth on her own. He had managed to prise the half full glass from her hand and already had a firm grip on her arm ready to lead her away when suddenly Mr Cray and Miss Lowe, both biology teachers, came over and, without realising the dangerous state his mother was in, Mr Cray involved her in the conversation, 'Mrs Fisher, so nice to see you. Miss Lowe and I were just discussing the problems of the rainforest and that most people are still not aware of the impact deforestation has on the whole fauna of the area'. 'Yes, chirped in Miss Lowe, I cannot stress enough how important it is that people should be made aware that by cutting down just one tree, thousands of species of insects are being robbed of their habitat and have to relocate and fight for survival – a hard battle many of them lose'. Charlie thought for a split second before deciding that it would probably be less embarrassing to just drag his mother away without excuse, even if she fell over in the process rather than letting her enter into a conversation with his teachers, but he had hesitated too long – his mother's reply was instantaneous. 'You are telling me that by cutting down a tree or a bush, you could actually mass murder insects?' she asked in a menacing tone. Mr Cray, immediately excited by the promise of a naïve but tentative listener, had quickly taken her captive and was setting off with her back to the hospitality tent. All Charlie could do was to join them in the hope that he might be able to avoid or at least repair any serious damage. Mr Cray complemented Sally on her grasp of the disastrous effects of deforestation, emphasising how he particularly liked her metaphor of 'mass murder' before continuing to unleash his passionate lecture on his victim. Alas, Sally had no intention of playing the listener. She had her own lecture to get off her chest and Mr Cray's enthusiasm was no match for Sally's because hers was driven by alcohol, not mere passion. 'Excuse me', Charlie heard his mother interrupting the teacher's sermon, 'this is very interesting for me because we have a little patio and there seem to be millions of these little buggers flying around. They've been annoying me for ages. We can't sit outside, we can't leave the door open in the evening and I often wondered why the fuck we have the bloody patio if we can't use it. But thanks to you, I know what to do now. I'll get rid of all the shrubs outside and cut down the tree at the bottom and that should do it!' Shocked and confused, Mr Cray, as if in a fit, let go of Sally's arm and, thankfully, Charlie was right beside his mother as she would surely have toppled over had he not got hold of her quickly. As he, once again, and this time successfully, manoeuvred her away from the drinks' stand, they left Mr Cray behind mumbling, 'Well, erm, well I', but clearly unable to find a response to Sally's interpretation of deforestation. As always, the next morning when she was almost sober, she would say, 'I hope I didn't embarrass you yesterday, darling?' And, as always, he would lie and say that she hadn't. To himself, he vowed however, that he would never let her set foot inside his school ever again.

* * *

But Sally found other ways of embarrassing her son, albeit unintentionally. She was determined to teach Charlie to be confident, no matter what. He was handsome and clever and should not have to feel a lesser human being just because he wasn't well off and didn't have a perfect family life. Every now and then, she would therefore insist that they went out together, either to the theatre or cinema, for afternoon tea or just for a stroll, depending on their finances. These outings were supposed to prove to everybody, including Charlie, that they led a normal life. In truth, it was Sally herself who needed affirmation, who needed to prove to herself that she was still able to fit within the boundaries of society. Last Thursday, Sally had decided that it was time for another tête-a-tête. The moment Charlie walked through the door that afternoon, he knew it was one of those days. There were distinctive signs that his mother had one of her sober interludes (which, to Charlie's relief was the only time she imposed these social lessons on him) – the curtains were drawn back, the windows open and there was a smell of home cooking. Sally announced over dinner that they were going to the cinema. Charlie never had a say in the matter as it depended entirely on his mother's condition, which was totally unpredictable, even for herself. As on all these occasions, Sally would dress in what she considered to be elegant. Charlie was not interested in clothes and had little knowledge of what was fashionable for women of his mother's age but he knew with as much certainty as he knew his own name that it was not what his mother was wearing. More often than not, he suffered the embarrassment quietly but there were times, like that Thursday, when he couldn't help himself. The bright red suit and non-matching red shoes he would have been willing to pretend to ignore, but the bird-nest-like hat in a different red altogether exceeded the boundaries of his well-tried and practised tolerance. 'Mum, don't wear that hat. Please!' 'Why not?' came the genuinely surprised response.

'Because it looks bloody stupid.'

'It's a very expensive hat, and I like it!'

'You look silly and it's embarrassing.'

'Don't be ridiculous, darling. You care too much about what other people think.'

'And you clearly too little.'

'You have to grow up and learn to stand up for what you believe.'

'Well, I believe you look stupid and I don't want to be seen with you!'

'That's ok, darling. But I disagree and I love this hat. It's vintage, made by a very famous designer and anybody who knows anything about fashion will recognise it.'

Charlie, unlike Sally, was not an argumentative person and he was aware that any further resistance on his part would just delay but not cancel his mother's plans for the evening. 'Ok, let's just go. My whole life you've embarrassed me and you're right – it's time I stopped giving a shit.' 'Language!', she reprimanded, seriously shocked, because whilst not shy about swearing herself, she had never tolerated it with Charlie.

They had only been walking for a few minutes and were about to turn into a side street when Charlie realised that they were being followed by two dubious looking men. He turned to his mother and whispered, 'I think we are going to be mugged'. 'What of', came the less than worried reply. 'Well, good luck to them!'

'Hey, you two', shouted one of the men. 'You look as if you have a big evening planned. Got some cash on you?'

'No, actually we don't', replied Sally calmly and truthfully as she hardly ever had cash on her. Her answer as well as her relaxed attitude agitated the man, 'Shut up, bitch and just hand over what's in your pocket!' Sally was not easily scared and for some reason she did not grasp the seriousness of their situation, 'Here, one clean, one dirty tissue – which one do you want? The muggers were not amused and were growing impatient, especially the one who had so far done all the talking. 'Don't try and be fucking funny, bitch!' It was only when Sally saw the knife in his hand that she changed her tone, 'Seriously, I've got nothing on me.' The second man suddenly turned to Charlie, 'What about you?'

Charlie too had seen the knife, 'Here is my mobile', he immediately offered.

'Jesus Christ, nobody uses this shit anymore. They're two fucking losers. I think I'll just slice them in half.

'Have my hat', Sally quickly suggested.

'You a fucking nutcase or what?'

'It's more expensive than the phone.'

'I don't want your fucking hat!'

But as he said this, he ripped the hat off her head, pulled it into several pieces which he then threw into the nearest puddle. Then, annoyed at the lack of loot, he raised his knife. Luckily, the second mugger was getting bored and also eager to move on to find more lucrative victims so he urged his companion to leave, 'Come on, we're just wasting time!' Looking at his knife, the first mugger took a second before he turned around and started to walk away from them shouting, 'This is your fucking, lucky day!'

As Sally and Charlie, still in shock (Charlie more so than his mother), carried on walking, Sally turned her head back, nodding towards the puddle, 'Did you arrange this?' she asked and they both burst out laughing. This experience, although scary, had created an atmosphere between them that was reminiscent of a time when mother and son had shared an extreme closeness and which now seemed so long ago. Afterwards, neither of them felt like going to the cinema anymore, and, despite Sally's dolled-up appearance, they agreed to visit their once favourite haunt. Sally loved this old, noisy iron bridge that seemed to laugh and cry with the wind and which divided the old city from its modern addition. There was nothing particularly beautiful about the bridge, its main attraction for Sally lay in the fact that it was deserted. The bridge had a much higher arch than the new one because it was built in the days when big trade ships had to pass underneath. The untamed river below always appeared louder and faster flowing here than anywhere else in the city. When Charlie was little, Sally used to tell him that the bridge and the river were talking to each other and she would make up these wonderful stories about their conversations. When he was five or six, they would argue which of the two was the wiser – the river because it was moving all the time and saw a lot of the world or the bridge which stood still but observed the changing of time. There are fifty seven steps to be climbed to get to the top of the bridge but it felt like a different world once they were up there. In the old days, the now modern part of the city used to be fields and meadows and then horse-drawn carts were allowed to cross over the bridge to transport produce to be sold in the market. But for many years now, the horse path was closed off and the bridge had only been accessible for pedestrians. Though hardly anybody used the old foot bridge anymore because most people preferred to cross over the elaborate and fashionably designed modern bridge further down. Before Charlie was born, Sally used to come here on her own. The sound of the river helped her relax and think clearly. In the last few years, she had only been here once or twice on her own because whilst the bridge held many happy memories for her, the realisation that these happy times were lost to her forever, upset her too much and had only resulted in increased alcohol consumption. But coming here with Charlie always felt good. It gave Sally the opportunity to indulge in her favourite pastime – pretence. She could, once more, pretend that everything would be alright.

For Charlie too, the old bridge held lots of happy childhood memories but unlike Sally, Charlie was no dreamer. So he only reluctantly accompanied his mother to the old bridge. For him, any memory of a happy past made the misery of the present more obvious. He did not want to be reminded of his happy, carefree childhood when he had a proper family life and money was aplenty; a time when his mother was the centre of his universe and when he loved her more than anybody else in this world because she was always there for him and she always understood him. Charlie did not want to remember the relationship he used to have with his mother because more and more lately, he would find an excuse to avoid any sort of conversation with her. Not just because he couldn't bear the constant repetition of her lies or because he didn't trust himself to control his frustration and not to shout the truth into her face, but mostly because he had started to loath her, how she looked and talked, how her breath reeked of alcohol most of the time. He was unable to forgive her for all the embarrassment she kept causing him.

* * *

Sally was at her most dangerous when only slightly inebriated. Once fully drunk, Charlie could handle her – he just needed to hold her firmly so she wouldn't keel over and then, at the first suitable location, lie her down flat to sleep it all off. Thankfully for Charlie, although it never ceased to amaze him, Sally was hardly ever sick, no matter whether she drank wine, beer or spirits and regardless of how much she consumed. However, during the early stages of drunkenness, Sally was aggressive and argumentative and nobody, not even Charlie, could control her. Naturally, Charlie tried to avoid her during these in-between stages but it wasn't always possible because it was particularly then, of course, that she was desperate for company. Not that she was ever aggressive towards Charlie, no, never, but she would insist, if he was around, that he should accompany her to wherever she suddenly decided she needed to go to. This was often a shop she'd been to before when sober, where something had annoyed her, maybe some shop assistant hadn't treated her properly but, due to the involuntary change in life style, without the influence of alcohol, Sally was easily intimidated. Once, just as Charlie was about to escape, she suddenly jumped up from the settee and shouted, 'Wait, I just broke a nail and I seem to have lost my nail file. I'll walk with you down to Rowley's'. Charlie knew it was pointless to attempt to wriggle out, he had tried too many times before and always failed.

So they went to their local department store where he had to play the loving, attentive, confident son who'd willingly accompany his mother shopping. Sally had marched through the automatic doors and gone straight towards a tall, blonde, very pretty looking girl in her mid-twenties. She stopped right in front of her and then turned round to Charlie, 'We are going to look for you in a minute, darling. I'll just quickly get this one thing.' Then she addressed the girl in her poshest voice and most charming, but unmistakably demanding tone, 'I'm looking for an emery board, darling'. 'They are just over there', came the bored, unhelpful, heavily accented, probably Eastern European, reply. Oh, the unsuspecting fool, thought Charlie as his mother asked sweetly, 'Would you mind terribly, darling, and bring one over? Just a very simple one. I've been out shopping all day, I'm absolutely exhausted!' Reluctantly and without another word, the girl sauntered off. Five minutes later she was shuffling back clutching an ironing board to her side. Whilst observing Sally's triumphant smile, Charlie was trying to decide whether he felt more sorry for the girl or himself. But at the sound of his mother's roaring laughter, he only cared about one thing – to get it over with and get out of there and he knew the best way to achieve this was by letting his mother finish her performance. Sally laughed until she had attracted a decently sized audience before starting her attack which ranged between ridiculing the girl to insulting all foreigners. She then finished off by turning to Charlie, 'Come on darling, let's go somewhere else. I don't want to waste any more time here'. So, mother and son would go back home together – she, content with her achievement … he, hating her more than ever.

* * *

When Matt walked out on them that evening, five years ago, Sally was only concerned about the effect it would have on Charlie. As for herself, she felt relieved because in her view, Matt had never been as committed to ensuring Charlie's happiness as she was. And whilst she was aware that Matt was often right when it came to financial matters and generally more sensible as far as all practical things were concerned, she often found him quite insensitive towards Charlie's or her feelings. Everything was matter of fact for Matt while for Sally, everything was a question of how it would affect Charlie. It could have been a perfect combination had the right balance been found. Alas, no balance was ever established because in the first few years of their marriage their wealth made any compromise unnecessary. Sally indulged Charlie because she loved him deeply and Matt indulged both of them because he could afford to. This is not to say that Matt didn't love his wife and son, he just did so according to his feasibility study. Many, many times when, although money was already in short supply, they could still have afforded the odd treat for Charlie, Matt had refused on the grounds that they had to keep some money back for emergencies. For Sally, however, it was always more essential, despite being less sensible, to see her son beaming with excitement. So, very often, she would then sell a piece of jewellery that she hadn't worn in ages in order to finance a little surprise present for Charlie and would tell Matt that she had helped out in the café round the corner which she actually did do occasionally.

After Sally had lost her part-time job as a receptionist because too often she didn't make it into work, she had basically become unemployable as far as normal jobs went. When, on top of that, the café round the corner had closed down and Matt had stopped sending any money at all claiming he was unable to support them anymore, Sally was left in dire straits. Unable to pay the rent and basic household bills, she went to see the bank manager to ask for a loan. At one time, they used to be very friendly with William Pope because for a while Charlie attended the same school as the Pope's son. So Sally had hoped that William would be sympathetic to her situation and help her. She was half right – William offered plenty of sympathy but sadly no help. What use were his lamentations of 'I'm so sorry to hear that Matt left' and 'You poor thing, I can't imagine what you are going through' when they were followed by ruthlessly sober statements like 'No bank will lend you any money if you have no income'. And to her reassurances that she would soon have another job, he just told her to come back when she did. Sally was not used to asking favours and she was very sensitive to the fact that her current situation forced her to do it. Throughout the whole meeting, she had felt that he couldn't wait to get rid of her. When she finally left, she felt humiliated and her problems were magnified to such proportion that it drove her to open a bottle of wine as early as eleven a.m. when normally she would not start drinking before two p.m. What would happen to them if she couldn't pay the rent? What would she tell Charlie why they had no electricity? After the first glass she already felt better and confident that something would turn up to improve their situation. After all, she still had two weeks to produce the money. By the end of the bottle, she didn't care about anything anymore. When she woke up and the realisation hit her that their situation would not improve by itself, she felt worse than ever. She battled with the temptation to open another bottle to combat the devastation and fear that raged within her. But luckily for Sally, desperation proved to be a perfect source of inspiration.

Not far from where they lived was a betting shop and Sally had often been surprised about how busy it seemed inside all day long, no matter what time she passed. So she took the last £50 out of the emergency tin and decided to try her luck betting. Other people did it and won, at least occasionally, and, so she argued, as long as she didn't bet much, she also couldn't lose much, but as long as there was a chance that she could actually make a profit, it was worth a try. Despite never having set foot inside a betting shop before, she was determined not to display any insecurity. After all, if there was one thing she was good at, it was pretence. Or so she thought.

Heart pounding, she bounced into the unknown. At first glance, she was pleasantly surprised because, although a bit dingy, it didn't seem as seedy as she had expected. Sally thought the large room with its counters and multiple screens resembled a mixture between a bank and an airport. There were about twenty men scattered around the room, gathered in little groups underneath the various screens, staring at the monitors – well, until Sally entered, that is, as then all forty eyes focused just on her. She didn't mind being looked at. For a minute or so she stood there motionless, receiving their glances with a confident smile. Sally was forty-five and lucky that the alcohol abuse of the last few years had not left more significant signs than a few wrinkles here and there which were easily camouflaged with the right make-up. Her body too was still in good shape. She was slim, not too tall but had long legs and her boobs were not too bad either – ok, they needed a little help to stay up there but neither did they droop to her knees once she removed the bra. She knew she could still look attractive and that day she had made a special effort. The short, tight, navy blue dress revealed a perfect cleavage and showed off all her assets without appearing vulgar.

Once her eyes had adjusted to the dim lighting, she slowly moved further into the room until she had found her target – a man on his own at the back of the room leaning against one of those high stands that can also be found in bars or banks. Like all the others, he too had stared at her but now that she was heading in his direction, he busied himself with filling in a card in front of him. 'Excuse me', she said in her sweetest, most relaxed voice although the thin, tight lips betrayed her display of confidence and joviality. 'Well, hello there', came the far too confident, far too provocative and far too loud reply. Taken aback, she whispered, 'I'm sorry but I've never placed a bet before … so I'm not quite sure where to start', sounding more helpless than she had intended to. He immediately picked up on her hushed tone and asked very quietly, 'So why on earth would you want to start now?' She leaned closer towards him, 'Because I need the money', she replied truthfully. As she moved back again, he made two steps towards her and breathed in her ear, 'There are other ways of making money, my dear', leaving no doubt as to which particular way he had in mind. Sally had always enjoyed a good flirt and, as she wanted his help, would not be a spoil sport now. With a fair amount of eye lash flutter and more than a hint of 'damsel in distress' symptoms in her voice, she uttered, 'Oh my, I think I'm past the sell-by date'. He fixed his eyes on hers whilst he put one finger on her thigh and slid it slowly up and down, 'I don't know', he whispered, 'I wouldn't mind paying to see more of these legs'. Suddenly, in Sally's mind, harmless flirt turned into a business opportunity, 'How much?' she asked sheepishly. Slowly, he scanned every inch of her body and Sally could feel her dress sticking to her as if she had been caught in the rain and found herself unable to stop the fire that was burning up her cheeks. But she kept her composure and a clear mind. So when he suddenly, with changed demeanour and matter-of-fact voice, mentioned £50, she was quick to fire back, 'Per leg?' He laughed, but only because he needed time to think. He had realised that he'd misjudged her – she was definitely no easy prey. Deciding on a more cautious approach he asked, 'How serious are you about making money?' Sally was pleased with the way she had handled the situation so far and was determined not to lose control, 'How serious are you about helping me?' 'I could help you to a steady income, more lucrative and more reliable than betting'. Now it was Sally's turn to think. Having at first believed that he was going to pay her to have sex with him and mentally weighed up that, as he wasn't bad looking and for the right price, it might well be worth the effort, she was now not sure anymore what he was proposing so she asked carefully, 'What did you have in mind?' He smiled, 'You really want me to spell it out?' She returned his smile, 'Yeah, please do.' He put his hand gently on her arm, 'Listen, you are gorgeous and most men in here would probably pay 100 quid for half an hour with you. Most of them won't even take that long. Nothing kinky, I'd make sure of that ... unless you're into that sort of thing, otherwise just straightforward, old fashioned stuff. These guys come here every day to escape their dreary reality and you'd make a great addition to their daily routine.' Although his voice had been quiet and soft, Sally could feel his hand on her arm tightening as he spoke. She looked him straight in the eye as she pulled her arm away from his grip, 'And you would be my pimp, I assume?' 'Employer', he protested grinning, 'I prefer employer. And I'm very reasonable, I only expect 20 percent of your daily takings. Believe it or not, I really do want to help you.' 'Yeah, she replied sarcastically, I can tell, you have a heart of gold. Where would all this take place?' He nodded his head towards a door behind them, 'There's a little room in the back with a sofa in it.' She automatically turned round whilst inquiring, 'What about the owner?' 'I am the owner', came the half expected reply.

And so, for a while, Sally had a steady income, with flexible working hours and free beverages. Her clients all turned out to be perfectly nice and Dave proved himself to be a really decent chap, never trying to cheat her and always behaving very pleasantly towards her. Financially, she was doing extremely well, earning well over a thousand pounds a week which enabled her to spoil Charlie, who had become more fashion aware, by buying him some nice clothes as well as taking him to more expensive restaurants. Charlie was led to believe that his mother worked in the customer services department of an on-line retailer. Sadly, after only a few months, an unfortunate incident forced Sally to terminate her 'customer services' employment.

* * *

One evening, at the theatre, Charlie and Sally bumped into Charlie's maths teacher. A strange looking man in his fifties – not outright ugly yet very unattractive. His hair was greasy and he had an old, unwashed smell about him. Charlie said he was extremely strict and had quite a vile temper, all the younger pupils were scared of him. So it was a big surprise when Mr Wilcox displayed perfectly charming manners. He praised Charlie's ability and complemented Sally on her parenting skills. Now, Sally was suspicious of anybody who was friendly to her, so when, whilst Charlie went to get himself some ice cream, Mr Wilcox sidled up to her with a nauseating smile on his face, Sally had a bad feeling. 'I understand you offer some special services, Mrs Fisher', he whispered. It had never occurred to Sally that her business in the betting shop would not stay secret. She was so perplexed by the unexpected proposition that 'Excuse me?' was all she could utter. 'Don't be coy, Mrs Fisher, everybody knows about your job at the betting shop. I just wondered if you did house calls?' Sally quickly decided that, as she hadn't been caught in the act, she would vehemently deny any allegation. 'I have no idea what you have heard or what you are insinuating', she snapped back. But Mr Wilcox was an obstinate man who did not give up easily once he had set his mind on something – and he had set his mind on Sally. He had lusted after her long before he'd even heard that it was possible to buy her services and he was determined not to miss his opportunity. He was of course aware that, him being Charlie's teacher, the situation was more delicate and so he was not surprised by Sally's denial and fully prepared for it. 'I spoke to Dave and he told me to drop in during morning break, at ten thirty. I only thought you might rather come …' but Sally did not let him finish his sentence, 'Whatever arrangement you've made does not involve me and has absolutely nothing to do with me. So focus your filthy mind elsewhere! How dare you insult me like this! I should report you to the school before you start to spread any rumours', she hissed at him indignantly. 'Too late for that my dear', he sniggered triumphantly, 'how do you think I heard about it?' Sally froze as he moved closer towards her until she was suddenly brought back into existence by a strong sense of nausea caused by his sour smelling body odour. 'Would you rather, Mrs Fisher, I made my appointment through Charlie', he asked threateningly. But before Sally could react, Charlie had returned with his ice cream and noticing the look of horror on his mother's face he asked, 'Everything alright?' 'Yes', she assured him, 'I just feel a little nauseous'. With the ringing of the bell, Mr Wilcox took his leave, humbly bowing to Sally, 'Such a pleasure, Mrs Fisher, I hope to see you again very soon'.

The next morning she hurried to see Dave and told him that she had to stop, at least for a while. Dave tried to prevent her from quitting. After all, the arrangement had also been very profitable for him – his betting shop was booming – not just because of the small percentage he took off Sally's fee but more so because men who would normally not have set foot in his establishment, came in to place bets whilst they were waiting for Sally to become available. But Sally reminded Dave of her original condition, namely that she had to approve any new customer. She had insisted on knowing the name of as well as seeing any potential client before consenting to render her services – all for the simple reason to avoid a 'Mr Wilcox' situation. Under no circumstances was her son to find out the truth about her job. Dave admitted his fault in not consulting her but, he said, Mr Wilcox was told by an existing customer. Dave promised Sally that he would sort it out – he'd get rid of Mr Wilcox and any indiscreet client so she'd have nothing to worry about in future. He even insisted that, if necessary, he'd employ her legitimately as admin staff if he had to. A month later, Sally returned to her old job where most of her previous clients were anxiously awaiting her. Sally never heard from Mr Wilcox again. Dave never mentioned how he sorted things out and Sally never asked but everything was again running smoothly and profitably.

* * *

Sally was earning plenty of money so she and Charlie lived comfortably, almost luxuriously. Sally was the closest to happy she had been for years. Dave had kept his promise and officially employed her as office help. Sally told Charlie that she had quit her job in customer services and now did admin work at the betting shop because the pay was a lot better. She was so convincing that she nearly believed it herself with the result that she even drank less these days. She had managed to invest a substantial amount of money which would be more than sufficient for Charlie's university education and on top of that, she had put enough cash aside to save up for a car for Charlie's eighteenth birthday, as he had recently passed his driving test. She was so excited when the big day finally arrived – 21st January, a Sunday. She had bought his favourite chocolate cake, a nice card and had put the car keys in a small box which she had neatly wrapped. A bottle of champagne was in the fridge for later after he had taken the new car for a spin. Sally had got up early and was sitting there readily dressed when Charlie emerged from his bedroom at about eleven. 'Happy Birthday, darling', she chirped as she got up to give him a hug. 'Thanks mum', came the still sleepy reply. Then, on seeing the cake, 'Oh, yum, you got my favourite cake!' He sat down and opened the card. Sally pushed the small box towards him and Charlie picked it up with raised eyebrows, 'Hmm, a present'. Sally kept her eyes fixed on him. She did not want to miss any of the surprise and joy that would shortly be displayed in his face because this was what she had lived for all her life, it was what she needed to breathe. Charlie took out the set of keys held together with the 'BMW' ring attachment, 'Is this a joke?', he asked in total disbelief. Sally burst out laughing with childish excitement, 'No, darling, it's not a joke! I bought you a car. Not brand new, but only three years old and in excellent condition. It's a BMW three series and I'm sure you will love it. Quickly, get dressed so that … 'No!' he shouted, 'I don't want it!' He flung the keys across the table as if they were poisonous. Sally, too shocked to be upset and assuming that he was just worried about the cost, stuttered, 'I can afford it, really. Don't worry, darling.'

'I know you can', came his hatred laden reply, 'But I don't want any of it. It is bad enough that I have to live here off your hard earned cash, I am not humiliating myself further by accepting expensive presents!' Not knowing where his anger stemmed from nor how to relate to it, Sally stammered, 'What's wrong? Why are you so upset?' He sneered at her, 'Let me make it clearer: I don't want any of your fuck money!' For several minutes, Sally did not respond, she could not think, she could barely breathe. The realisation that he knew the truth about her job had knocked the very life out of her. 'How long have you known?', she whispered at last. He shook his head, 'What does it matter', came the frustrated reply, 'Whether I have known for years or only since yesterday? In the same way that it doesn't matter if you worked as a whore for a day or for years! Just don't be so bloody proud of how much you've earned!' Disgust was written all over his face. Unable to bear his look any longer, Sally got up and turned away from him. 'But I did it all for you!', she said almost involuntarily. And as this phrase, so anchored in her mind for years, was for the first time made audible, she realised before she had even finished speaking, how absolutely absurd it must sound to him. She didn't need to look at him to know that he felt nothing but utter contempt for her. And who could blame him? Did what for him? Enable him to have a miserable life? Because that is all he can see, all he remembers – misery. He lives in the present, and that's all he judges by. The past, his happy childhood is irrelevant. He wants to be happy now and all he knows is that he can't. She loves him so much, idolises him and yet, she ruined his life. Maybe he could cope with the present if only he had a future to look forward to. Young people live for the moment but they like to dream about the future. It is easier to cope with upsets and disappointment if there is something to look forward to in the future. Anticipation and goal – that's what's important. Something worth living for, something to make it worth putting up with a shitty today! Charlie did not have that right now. She, on the other hand, always had a reason to carry on, something to look forward to – Charlie was her anticipation and his happiness her goal. So why did it go so wrong? How could she have made so many wrong choices for all the right reasons? She only did what most parents do for their children – she tried to protect him, spoil him, give him the best possible start in life. But she had failed. She knew she had ruined his life, with her obsession to indulge him because she could not bear to see him wanting, with her obsession to see him happy because his happiness was her fulfilment, she ruined his life with her love. Or was it selfishness, she wondered.

Can love make one both selfless and selfish at the same time? It was true, although it sounded like a cliché now, everything she ever did was out of love for him. His happiness was the only profit she desired and his love the only thing she'd ever hoped for. The only reason she started drinking was because she couldn't bear to see him unhappy after Matt left, couldn't cope with failing him. But she came good, found a job, provided for her son and for a little while she genuinely believed she would achieve her goal and see her son content and happy after all. Alas, Charlie was more miserable now than ever and he hated her.

* * *

Charlie knew how much he had hurt her with his harsh words and by not accepting the car, by spoiling the joy she took in surprising him. And he already regretted his outburst by the time he had slammed the door behind him. He felt sorry for her. He did not want the car, no way, but he could have handled it differently. He was annoyed with himself for mentioning that he knew about her job in the betting shop. He had known for a while and lived with it, there was no need to tell her now, it would not change anything, just hurt and embarrass her because she had tried so hard to keep it from him. But the car was just so unexpected, it was too much for him, he could not bear the humiliation of accepting such an expensive present funded entirely by prostitution – he found it sickening, and so he'd snapped. For years, Charlie had been torn between the love for his mother that was so deeply rooted inside him that it would dampen even the worst anger he felt for her, and his growing hatred for her ridiculous actions and drunken behaviour which seemed to have got worse from when he first became aware of them and then steadily increased the older he got. But lately, he had found that these diverse emotions were ceasing to battle with each other. His feelings had reached a point of neutrality as they were slowly diminishing on either side. He still loved his mother and always would but not in that painful way where it would hurt so badly when she made a fool of herself, when others talked and laughed about her. Similarly, he got less upset and frustrated when she 'misbehaved'. Whilst strolling along, he even found himself amused as he remembered some of the things she had put him through. He was thinking about his forthcoming university life and then let his mind drift back to his school years and the dreadful time he had had, except he did not feel sorry for himself like he used to, and when he suddenly recalled this vision of his inebriated mother in her tight leather skirt and see-through blouse, looking extremely sexy and not unattractive but totally inappropriate for a school's parents' evening and telling his arts teacher that he was about as creative as a three-legged donkey followed by an apology to the donkey which she didn't mean to insult, just because the man had dared to tell her that her son's latest project was not 'A' quality, Charlie, at the memory of it, could not help but smile to himself. She was quite a character, his mother. He knew she had tried, for his sake, to fit within the social parameters of a middle class bourgeois society. He also knew that she had failed because she had tried too hard and cared too much. He had learned over the years not to care what people said or thought about him, not just for self-preservation but because he had realised that one was more likely to be accepted, even respected, by society if one didn't give a hoot. And what the fuck was society anyway but a bunch of hypocrites? Charlie, like

Sally, liked walking, it gave him the feeling that he was turning his back on bad things and enabled him to restore control over his life.

* * *

Sally's binge had lasted longer than normal but when she finally emerged from it, she did so with a clear idea in mind of how to solve all Charlie's problems and to sort out, once and for all, a happy future for him. She would not fail this time. Since his birthday, she had hardly seen him or talked to him but today she would cook dinner and then tell him that all will be ok. First, she had to return the car, then she would go and tell Dave that she will no longer work for him. As Charlie unlocked the front door that evening, he knew immediately by the smell that greeted him from the kitchen that his mother had entered into a sober phase. He was only partly pleased because it meant that he had to talk to her and that she would most probably address the birthday incident. But Sally surprised him by being unusually quiet during the meal. When she suggested going for a walk after dinner to the old bridge, Charlie didn't want to refuse her. After walking a few minutes in silence, she seemed to suddenly come to life, sheltered by the darkness, and told him how sorry she was that she was responsible for his miserable life. 'It wasn't all bad', he gently protested. But Sally knew it was just a weak attempt to try and make her feel better, so she ignored it and carried on with what she was determined to tell him. 'No matter how sorry I am about the past, I cannot change it. But I can make sure that you have a happy future. I have found a solution. Finally, I know exactly what to do. I have it all worked out. And I promise I shall never again cause you any embarrassment!' As always when she was excited, Sally talked very quickly, hardly pausing for breath so as not to allow a response from her listener. She needn't have worried, Charlie was a practised listener, he knew the rules. So, with a frozen smile on his face, he trudged quietly alongside her and let her ramble on until she had got it all off her chest, after which she would feel better, less guilty. He could do that for her, at least that, to make her feel happier. It didn't even matter that he hadn't heard half of what she was saying, as long as she believed she had an audience. Once she had completed her mission, they usually had quite a nice time discussing various topics or just reminiscing, and she could be quite funny. He had to admit, his mother, when relaxed and at ease, had a good sense of humour. He had always appreciated that. 'You really mustn't worry about me', he heard her say, 'I have sorted everything out and I am so happy about it. And you will have the best time at university – that's the only thing you have to promise me'. 'Ok, mother', he laughed, aware that this marked the end of her lecture.

They walked up the fifty seven steps to the top of the bridge accompanied by light-hearted banter. There was something Charlie had wanted to ask his mother for a long time but had never found the right opportunity. As they were standing there, holding on to the railings whilst trying to catch their breath from the climb, Charlie wondered if now might be the right time. He was worried though that his question might upset her and draw her straight back into depression. He glanced at her sideways, then put his hand on hers, 'Mum, I'd like to ask you something', he said hesitantly. Sally would not have denied him anything right now – it had been ages since he had shown her such affection. She was so deeply touched by his gesture that she struggled to fight back her tears. Charlie, misinterpreting her silence, added, 'but if you don't want to talk about it, you don't have to answer'. 'Ask me anything you like', she finally said, 'and I shall answer truthfully. 'Mum', what really happened to dad? Why has he never contacted me?' Sally turned round and faced her grown up, handsome son, searching his eyes to find out how much of the truth he'd be able to cope with. He was a head taller than her and she had to tilt her head back to be able to lock her eyes with his. 'For a while, after he left us, your father had a very rough time – no money, no job, nowhere to live. He stayed with a cousin for a few weeks until social services had sorted out a place for him. He was too embarrassed in the beginning to face you so we agreed on that story of him working abroad'. As she spoke, she started to notice a flicker of concern and disbelief in his look and a hint of cynicism flashing over his otherwise pursed lips. The truth, that's what she had promised him. But did he really need to know it? What was the point in telling him that his father did not want to see him because not only did he not care enough about him, he actually despised him – Matt considered Charlie to be the reason for his misery. He blamed Charlie for their financial ruin and their marriage break-up. Matt had always resented the love and devotion Sally had shown her son and he grew jealous of the ever increasing bond between them. Matt was fighting Charlie for Sally's attention and he was losing. In the end, he had felt like an outsider. Rather than the bitter truth, Sally decided to tell Charlie what she had rehearsed many times in her head in preparation for this question, knowing that it would one day be asked. 'Once you had stopped asking about your dad, we decided it was better he wouldn't contact you until you were quite a bit older. We didn't want to upset you again, you had suffered so much already'. 'It doesn't make sense', Charlie interrupted,' not if he cared for me at all'. Sally, no matter how much she hated Matt right now, would make him look good and caring for Charlie's sake. 'It's not because he didn't love you, darling but because he loved you too much. He could not bear to see you upset. And goodness knows, I know how hard it is to see you unhappy and not being able to do anything about it'. 'But you did not run away', he replied angrily, turning away from her so that she couldn't see his eyes welling up. 'I'm stronger, less sentimental', she replied. And this was absolutely true – whilst highly emotional and temperamental, Sally was a very down-to-earth person who had no time for sentimentality. In fact, she was quite a cynic, with no romantic tendencies. She always sneered at people who'd say 'Oh, this is where he first proposed' or 'this is where we first made love'. Not that she'd never loved Matt, of course she did, actually she was very much in love with him in the beginning but marriage, well, that was more for practical reasons, security and all that. Sally, encouraged by his earlier gesture, put her arm on Charlie's shoulder, 'We all do the wrong things at times for the right reasons.' 'Where is he now? Are you still in contact with him?', he inquired further. 'The last time I heard from him was five years ago when he wanted a divorce so he could get remarried and move to Australia', she told him, sounding more resentful than she had intended to. She couldn't have cared less about the divorce or him remarrying, but she was very upset at the time about Matt's lack of concern for Charlie and his unwillingness to provide any financial support when he clearly had enough money to emigrate. 'I'm sorry, mum', Charlie answered, misunderstanding her resentment. Realising his concern, she replied quickly 'Oh, there was not much love lost between your father and me. The only thing we had in common was our love for you.' He frowned, 'You must have loved each other once? What happened?' A flicker of a smile softened her face, 'You know how, in science, opposites attract and positives will repel each other? Well, your dad and I were both positive, I was happy, he was happy and together we were unhappy'.

He laughed, 'Shame you never met my physics teacher'. She playfully slapped his arm, 'Well, you know what I mean. We were just not compatible but it took us a while to realise it and a little while longer to admit and act on it. It became more obvious after he had lost his job and spent more time at home.'

'I was really upset about dad leaving because deep down I knew that he would not come back. I just wanted so much to believe your story about his job abroad. It took me a long time to come to terms with it. I sometimes wonder if it had been better to have been told the truth from the beginning, rather than having to piece it together myself.'

'I did so many things wrong, ruined so much for you in my quest to protect you from the truth which, you are right, might have been easier on you. All the damage I caused … for the sake of love.' He smiled, 'And out of love, I let you'. To hear that he loved her was more than she had expected and made her decision to set him free even easier. 'It's getting chilly', he broke the indulging silence, 'We should be heading back'. She looked at him with that grateful, admiring look that was reserved only for him, 'Do you mind if I stay for a little longer, I'd like a few minutes on my own. You head back, put the kettle on.' He smiled and nodded, his eyes so calm and relaxed as if he had just woken from a deep, comforting sleep.

She waited a few minutes after he had gone, cried a little as she thought of him opening her letter but all the while determined to execute her plan that would ensure his happiness. She was so pleased with her decision and so convinced that it was the best for him that she didn't feel the cold, didn't feel fear. She jumped with such ease and grace in the knowledge that the icy cold below promised both her salvation and his freedom. 'If only he knew how happy I am right now', she thought, 'he would not mourn me'.

He was almost half way down the stairs when it occurred to him, that he should let her know that he was happy, that, for the first time in his life, he was looking forward to tomorrow, ready to embrace his future. He decided to wait for her and sat down on the cold, rough stone steps, looking down into the roaring river. The wind and the moonlight had teamed up to create eerie shapes floating through the air and bouncing on top of the waves. And yet, he knew instinctively by the elegant movements of the drifting object, so still yet so alive until it hit the raging waves. 'Noooooooo', he screamed with every fibre of his being.

JUST POPPING OUT

'I'm just popping out to get the paper', he shouted upstairs, 'Maybe have the car washed and put some petrol in. Won't be long. An hour max!'

'Ok, I'll hop in the shower quickly', she replied. Kate loved her showers, especially at weekends when she didn't have to rush and there was no need to get dressed straight after. Coming out of the hot, steamy bathroom always made her feel chilly though and very sensitive to drafts. And on this icy and windy winter morning she could not just feel the cold air sweeping over her damp body but, she was convinced, even hear the wind whistling through the house. This could only mean one thing – her husband had once again forgotten to close the window in the sitting room when he left. So annoying. It was freezing outside. She now had to put on her bathrobe and run downstairs to close the window before she could continue to pamper herself. To her surprise, the window was closed. But there was a definite draft coming from somewhere.

She went into the long, narrow hall and was about to turn right into the kitchen when she realised that the front door was wide open. Assuming Pete had already come back, she shouted to him to hurry and close the door, but as she got nearer she realised that the car was still gone. Great! He'd forgotten that the latch was broken and the front door didn't stay shut unless properly locked. And of course, the locksmith can't come until Monday which meant one of them, probably her, would have to take half a day of work. Just because Pete insisted on using the same chap who'd done some work for him in the office for apparently being so reliable, trustworthy and cheap! Had it been up to her, she would have rung an emergency service, paid the extra call out fee and it would have been fixed by now. To think that she was upstairs in the shower whilst the front door was wide open! She quickly took the spare set of keys out of the cupboard drawer and locked the front door. Kate contemplated for a second whether she should leave the key in the lock so that Pete couldn't let himself back in, just to teach him a lesson, but concluded that it would be childish. So she threw the keys back in the drawer and hurried to the kitchen to get some fruit juice to take upstairs whilst continuing her weekend beauty ritual.

She didn't notice him. He stood in front of the patio door next to the tumble dryer. 'Orange juice would be nice', he said just as she was about to open the fridge. She let out a scream. Slowly she turned round, terrified to face the unfamiliar voice. 'Did you enjoy your shower,' he asked smilingly, clearly relishing her anxiety. How long, she thought, had this stranger been in my house? Had he been upstairs? Watched her in the shower? Stay calm ... and think, she told herself. Pete will be back shortly. But all she could think of was that she'd idiotically locked the front door and thus made any attempt of a quick escape impossible. She poured the orange juice, desperately trying to stop her hands from shaking. Damn! The carton was almost empty. He moved towards her and took the half full glass off her looking questioningly at the mean contents.

She grabbed the opportunity. 'I'll get some more from the garage', she offered. But as she turned round, he was leaning across the doorway. 'Not necessary', he grinned sarcastically. Kate's heart pounded frantically. She was trapped. She had to try and distract him ... or make him believe that somebody could walk through the door any minute. 'Oh, you must be Paul', she finally invented, trying to sound as casual as possible, 'My husband said you'd drop by this morning. He should be back any minute. I think he is back now, I just heard the car come into the driveway.'

But he did not budge. He did not seem affected at all by her announcement. 'I don't think your husband will be back too soon. It's not that quick to have a flat tyre fixed. And no, I'm not Paul.'

Oh no, she thought, he had planned this, watched the house, slashed the tyre. But what did he want? She realised, she was standing too close to him. Instinctively, she tightened her bathrobe. She had to get him away from the doorway. 'Why don't you sit down', she suggested in an attempt to get him as far away from the door as possible.

He declined with a cheeky grin. 'Are you hungry', she asked eying the bread knife that was lying next to the toaster. 'I could make you some toast.'

'Maybe afterwards', he replied whilst moving towards her holding out his empty glass. Panic stricken she snatched the bread knife and plunged it into him. As he collapsed, he tried to grab hold of her arm but she pushed him aside and ran to the front door. Whilst she fumbled for the keys in the drawer, the door bell rang. Thank God, she thought, Pete is back. 'Pete', she screamed hysterically as she opened the door, 'A man! A Man!'

'You mean, Kevin', he said puzzled by his wife's excitement, 'The locksmith? I ran into him at the petrol station and begged him to fix our lock today. I told him you might be in the shower so I gave him my keys. Didn't he tell you I had a flat tyre and would be a bit longer?'

ADULT EDUCATION

Liz thoroughly enjoyed the ten minute walk to the university but couldn't help wondering if it would hold the same charm in the middle of the winter, or indeed, in a few weeks' time once the novelty had worn off. The start of a new life was accompanied by both excitement and trepidation in equal measure. She smiled to herself as she remembered the disbelief in her children's faces when she confronted them with her decision to move to Cambridge in order to return to full time education. What bothered her most was that they weren't so much concerned about her but took objection to the fact that she hadn't consulted them first! Why should she? She hardly ever saw them these days – they visited about once a month and, if they needed something, might ring in between. Yet, they expected to be involved in decisions regarding her life!

As she walked through the massive entrance of the psychology faculty, she suddenly felt extremely nervous and seeing all these young people hanging around only increased her insecurity. One of these youngsters decided to leave his group of friends and headed right towards her: 'Hi, you seem a bit lost. Are you looking for someone?' How charming, she thought, but his young, handsome face and broad smile prevented her from admitting the truth. Liz was sixty five, healthy, energetic and attractive, and everybody told her she didn't look a day beyond fifty – at the moment, however, she felt like ninety five. She smiled politely, 'I'm fine, thank you very much', then walked swiftly along the draughty corridor and up the first flight of stairs, not knowing where she was heading. Of course, she was aware of how silly she was being. Before applying for the course, she had thought about it realistically, accepted that the majority of students would be a lot younger than her and even that there was a high chance that she would be the oldest student ever to attend a lecture. But she didn't mind, at least not in theory; in fact, it had somehow appealed to her eccentric nature ... except at this moment when it seemed that she had overestimated her resilience when it came to dealing with the reality of the situation. She was leaning against the banister trying to get her palpitations under control and hoping to stop perspiring before continuing her search for the lecture room.

Once she had calmed down and regained her composure, she had no problem in finding room 262 – for her first lecture in forty five years! The room was smaller than she'd expected it to be, otherwise it looked quite old fashioned which was somewhat comforting, well, until the nice, charming, smiley chap from earlier plonked himself right next to her. 'So that's what you were looking for! Room 262. See, you should have asked me!' Liz had no idea why she felt so embarrassed. It seemed that his immense confidence totally undermined hers. But there is one benefit to age – years and years of practice – so she was well rehearsed in the art of pretending, 'Looks like I found it without you ... and even beat you to it', she replied with most convincing superiority. 'My name is Paul'. She took his outstretched hand, 'Liz'. 'So', he asked, 'What other modules have you chosen?' Liz was in the process of explaining that she had decided to attend a fair amount of the undergraduate lectures just to trigger her memory, 'Well, it's been a while ...', when the lecturer, a woman half Liz's age, had started to put up the link for today's lecture on the big screen whilst already talking about the first topic and Liz was grateful not to have to continue her conversation with Paul.

The days passed quickly and already by the end of the first week her encounters with Paul seemed less daunting. It had got easier once the truth was out – that she was a very mature student – which didn't bother Paul, or indeed any of the other students, in the slightest. Paul was an extremely charming, courteous and helpful young man who clearly liked her company. Maybe, Liz thought, he saw her as a mother figure. Perhaps he didn't have a good relationship with his own mother or she may even be dead. One day she will find out. During the next few weeks Liz grew quite fond of Paul and looked forward to their daily meetings. They would often have lunch together and discuss their lectures, assignments, politics or just simply gossip or, which happened more and more lately, flirt – harmless, of course, and, at least as far as Liz was concerned, meaningless fun. One day, Paul greeted her with raised eyebrows and a far too loud, 'You're looking very sexy today!' She laughed it off replying, 'Gee, I never thought of my grandmother as being sexy, so … thank you!' 'Maybe she wasn't', came his immediate reply. But, although she didn't take it seriously for one moment, his comment did make her feel good. Well, who doesn't like flattery! Whilst she didn't put any real meaning to these flirtations, they did however prevent her from inviting him to her house. Not that her feelings towards him were anything but platonic, she just didn't want to worry and scare him by misinterpreting her intentions. An absurd idea, of course, after all she could theoretically be his grandmother! On the other hand, there are plenty of women who lust after young men – so, in order to avoid confusion, better stick to day-time rendezvous in public places.

The attention Paul paid Liz did not go unnoticed by his friends and the teasing started soon after their first encounter with comments ranging from 'Hi gigolo' when he entered a room to 'granny's here' the moment Liz appeared on the horizon. Paul didn't seem to mind though. He usually joined in and even encouraged it. This was, of course the right approach to deflate their mockery and it was due to this jolly attitude that Paul remained a solid member within his group of friends. On top of which, he went out partying as usual and had various flings with girls his own age. Paul was very popular and nothing, it seemed, could change that. Both boys and girls liked his company because he was clever, witty, charming, helpful and great fun. That he was also very attractive increased his chances with girls – he never seemed short of a sleeping companion! Girls usually saw him as a trophy and a personal triumph to be noticed by him and generally accepted that his interest in them would last just that one night. Occasionally however, and despite his well known reputation, girls were disillusioned or got jealous. A few weeks ago, Paul showed some interest in a pretty brunette English student named Rita and asked her out for a drink with the usual expectation of one passionate night. He told his friends the next day that Rita had got the wrong idea and was rather upset that he didn't want to arrange another date with her. He said that he was worried about her behaviour and warned his friends that she might approach them to complain about him. By the morning, she'd seemingly come to her senses but, as Paul predicted, she did try to talk to his friends, and even accused Paul of rape. His friends of course dismissed the ridiculous claim and had no sympathy for somebody who tried to make their friend look bad. They just told her to stop lying, 'Don't be absurd, girls are lining up to sleep with him. And we saw you making out in the bar, you couldn't get off with him quick enough!'

Before Rita there was one other girl who found it difficult to cope with Paul's flippant attitude. She walked around long-faced and tearful for days and told everybody that Paul was not the nice person he pretended to be. But eventually she got over it, once she realised that nobody was listening. Paul was very understanding and asked his friends to be nice to her, saying that he really didn't mean to hurt her and he felt truly sorry to have upset her. Had he been aware that she was looking for more than just a night of fun, he would never have asked her out. Liz hadn't failed to notice how popular Paul was nor did she miss the admiring glances girls gave him whenever he entered a room. When she first met him, she was surprised that he didn't have a girlfriend and even thought that he might be gay. As she got to know him a little, she realised that that wasn't the case. In fact, the better she knew him, the more obvious it became to her that the reason why Paul didn't have a girlfriend was because he liked variety and wanted to keep his options open. Well, Liz didn't think there was much wrong with that as long as all parties understood that and nobody got hurt. But good luck to the poor girl who tried to pin him down! She once asked him if he had ever had a proper girlfriend. He laughed then asked if sleeping with the same girl twice qualified.

As the weeks went by, Liz and Paul's relationship was widely accepted and it was generally believed that the two were a couple because they were always seen together – at lectures, at lunch, hanging out in the afternoon, either in town or sometimes even in Paul's room at his college. Occasionally, Paul would still go out with his friends and he would continue sleeping around. Nobody would ever mention this to Liz because first of all, apart from Paul, hardly any of the other students talked to her that much and secondly because it was assumed that she was fully aware of what Paul was up to and that she was probably even happy for him to have his fun, like a mother enjoyed watching her child play with his favourite toy. For weeks, everything seemed to be going really well. The other evening however, when Paul appeared in the common room, he was not his usual jolly self. He explained to his friends that he wanted to end his relationship with Liz but was worried about her reaction. Everybody assured him that she'd be fine because surely she must know that it was inevitable, that she couldn't possibly have expected the relationship to last forever and quite frankly, she was lucky that it lasted for as long as it had. Paul told them that he had tried to finish it a couple of weeks ago but she'd become hysterical so he'd promised to think about it for another week. Apparently they'd arranged to have a proper talk the next day at Liz's house and Paul was extremely worried because he hadn't changed his mind about breaking up but wasn't looking forward to a repetition of his previous attempt. And from the account he gave to his friends, he had all reason to be worried. He said she'd behaved totally irrationally, had threatened him with all kind of things and generally drifted into a state of sheer hysteria. His friends suggested that one of them should accompany him but Paul declined the offer saying it would be unfair to Liz because she would be embarrassed and besides, it would make him feel like a coward. No, no, he assured his friends that it's his mess and he alone had to find his way out of it.

Paul got up early the next morning to go for his run as usual. There were no lectures that day so he took his time over breakfast and had a long shower. A couple of his friends poked their heads round the corner to wish him good luck with granny, others had sent him emails first thing in the morning with similar messages. Paul was in no hurry, he wanted time to prepare himself for his encounter with Liz and had no intention of turning up on her doorstep before five pm. He spent a couple of hours working on his essay before going for lunch in the buttery, after which he strolled into town to do some shopping, buying a new shirt at Diesel with vouchers Liz had given him for his birthday. He went back to his room to freshen up and change into his new shirt before hopping on his bike at a quarter to five. He knocked on Liz's front door at five on the dot, much to Liz's surprise, 'Hi! … Erm … erm, what are you doing here? How do you even know where I live?'

'Not from you, that's for sure! I have a friend who lives not far from here and as I cycled past I saw your car so I stopped. You actually live here or are you visiting somebody?'

'I live here … it's easier if my kids want to come and visit. Oh … erm … do you want to come in?'

'I thought you'd never ask!' As he walked in he took a good look around, 'Very nice!'

'Yes, thank you. When I first saw it, I fell in love with the charming front garden and porch. And it still gives me pleasure every day I come home. You want some tea or a cold drink?'

'Hot or cold, I don't mind as long as it has vodka in it'.

'Isn't that a bit strong for this time of day?'

'What, in case I fall off my bike? Don't worry, a few vodkas won't have any effect on me. I'm chairman of my college's drinking society so … I've had lots of practice'.

'Ok, if you say so. Vodka and coke? Ice and lemon?'

'Great! Thanks!'

Paul threw himself on the sofa and when Liz came back with the drink she found him stretched out on it. 'Just make yourself comfortable', she said smiling at him.

Patting the sofa, Paul replied cheekily, 'I thought I'd try it out … in case I can't cycle back after all'.

Liz, although laughing, was determined that he should understand that staying over was not an option, 'In that case, don't gulp it down because one drink is all you are going to get'.

'You sure know how to make a guy welcome. ... But seriously now, why couldn't I stay the night? What are you worried about?'

'It wouldn't look right – you and I leaving here together in the morning ... it would send the wrong message'.

'And what message would that be?'

'The wrong one!' Liz was starting to feel uncomfortable and decided to change the subject, 'So where does your friend live?'

'Which one?'

'The one you just came from, the one you said lives near here'.

'Erm ...', Paul hesitated whilst keeping his eyes firmly fixed on Liz, 'I lied ... I followed you last time you walked home'.

'Why?'

'I wanted to know where you lived ... and you never invited me round so I thought maybe you have a reason ... maybe you don't live alone or something'.

'You could have just asked. But now you mention it, there is a reason why I hadn't asked you round ... namely, to avoid awkward situations ... like this'.

'I don't find it awkward'.

'Well, I do'.

'Why?' he asked teasingly, 'Are you worried that something might happen?'

'No, just worried that you might think that I would want something to happen'.

'And would you?'

'Certainly not', she replied firmly, 'I like you, Paul ... very much ... as a friend, to talk to ... that's all. And the reason I haven't invited you round is so that you wouldn't get the wrong idea'.

The smile had disappeared off Paul's face and he was now staring at her accusingly, 'But it's obviously on your mind'.

The change in Paul's demeanour had not escaped Liz and so she deliberately softened her tone to diffuse the situation, 'Only because I don't want you to think that I'm after you for anything else but because I enjoy your company ... and I'm a bit concerned about what other people think about our strange relationship'.

Paul suddenly jumped up and sat down next to her, 'I don't care what other people think ... I'm surprised you do, considering you totally changed your life at your age which to most people must seem absolutely crazy'.

'This is different ...'

'How? People gossip anyway – whether I'm walking out of here in half an hour or tomorrow morning'.

'You are right. I know. Still, there's a huge difference in visiting somebody for an hour in the afternoon or spending the night. You might not care what people think but you can't tell me that it never crossed your mind that people might not believe that our relationship is purely platonic?'

'Oh, I know most people think we are a couple and have hot sex every night'.

Liz felt more uncomfortable and alarmed by the minute, 'Oh my God! Is that what they say behind our backs? Has anybody mentioned anything to you directly ... like any of your friends?'

'Constantly', he answered matter of factly.

'Oh no, that's awful! Why didn't you say anything? I can't believe you don't mind'.

'All I mind is that they are not right'.

'I know', she agreed with him, 'To be accused of something that bears no relation to the truth ... it's just terrible! We must put them right'.

'That's not what I meant', he replied coldly, 'I'd rather they were right'.

'What?', she asked puzzled. Then, as she realised what he meant, 'Have you been drinking before you came here?'

'What, for courage? I don't need a drink for that'.

'No, why would you need courage? Stop it, Paul, this is starting to be too weird ... I think we should change the subject for now', and in an attempt to lighten up the situation she added half jokingly, 'and unless we can have a normal conversation, I shall have to ask you to leave ... and shall never invite you back'.

She was about to get up to escape the intense atmosphere when Paul suddenly put his hand on her breast, 'You don't get it, do you?'

Liz was terrified, 'Oh my God, Paul, stop! I told you, I never looked at you in this way, please, you don't understand ...'

But Paul could not be reached anymore. He threw himself on top of her and started to rip open her blouse panting, 'You are the one who doesn't understand ... I will fuck you whether you want to or not'.

Liz tried to protect herself, tried to fight him off, shouted at him, 'Ouch, ouch, you are hurting me, stop! Stop now! For God's sake get off me!'

But he did not stop. In fact, he became more violent. Panic stricken, Liz pushed him as hard as she could and, surprised by the sheer force, he fell backward onto the table. Liz jumped up but before she could turn round to run outside, she noticed the pool of blood by Paul's throat – he had fallen backwards onto the glass on the table and cut his artery. 'Oh my God! Paul! Paul! Talk to me, please!'

Liz realised that Paul was in danger of bleeding to death. She ran for a towel and pressed it against his throat with one hand whilst pushing some of the glass splinters away from his head. She reached for her phone and called an ambulance. Minutes later, the door bell rang. She let go off the towel and ran to open the door, 'Quickly, he is going to bleed to death!' One of the paramedics checked Paul's pulse, 'It's too late'. Liz broke down, crying uncontrollably, 'Oh no, please God, no!'

Despite explaining the accident to the two constables who turned up at her house, Liz was taken to the police station to answer some 'formalities'.

'So, again. You weren't expecting Mr Townsend to visit you that day and he had never been to your house before? Is that right?'

'Yes'.

'And you met Mr Townsend the first day you arrived at the university?'

'Correct'.

'You said you became very good friends in these last few months, is that right?'

'Yes, we got on extremely well. He is ... erm was such a charming boy ... so nice and helpful'.

'And yet, you had never invited him to your home? Why not?'

'I didn't want him to get the wrong idea'.

'About what?'

'I really liked him ... as a person, you know. I didn't want him to think that I was after him ... for any other reason'.

'You didn't fancy him then?'

'No! Certainly not ... I could have been his grandmother, for goodness' sake!'

'So why would you be worried then that he might think of you as anything else but a good friend?'

'I wasn't ... well, not at first ... I don't know ... maybe I was just worried about what other people might think.'

'And that didn't worry you during all the time you spent with him at university, for lunches, going out to dinner or drinks?'

'No, it didn't ... because there were always other people around.'

'And you didn't mind what these other people were thinking about your relationship?'

'I guess I never really thought about it.'

'Did Mr Townsend ever give you any indication that he might have certain desires for you?'

'No ... well ... not directly ... and certainly not in the beginning ... it's just that ... well, lately I thought ... and particularly now, in retrospect ... that his behaviour had changed slightly .... But it was all done jokingly and ... '

'For instance? Can you give me an example?'

'Well, erm, a couple of weeks ago I wore this green dress and he commented on how sexy I looked.'

'Had you worn that dress before?'

'No, it was new.'

'Was the dress more revealing than anything you would normally wear?'

'Maybe ... I guess ... because it's a summer dress.'

'Did you buy it specially for your meeting with Mr Townsend?'

'No! I bought it because I felt like treating myself and because

I hadn't been clothes shopping for ages ... and I hadn't brought too many summer dresses with me'.

'But you obviously wore it with the intention of looking attractive'.

'Everybody wants to look good ... most women make an effort ... '

'And you don't think that this effort, as you call it, to look good might have been made specially for Mr Townsend?'

'I'm not sure I understand what you are implying? You think I dressed to get his attention? Are you suggesting that I tried to seduce him?'

'Were you? ... Subconsciously, maybe?'

'No! No, I wasn't. I have children older than him! It would never have occurred to me to think of Paul as anything but a nice kid who, strangely enough, I got on really well with'.

'Why strangely?'

'What?'

'Why do you think it strange that you got on well with Mr Townsend?'

'Exactly for the same reason I just mentioned – he is younger than my own children, an undergraduate student, and yet I managed to have some very serious conversations with him which resulted in a very mature friendship'.

'So you didn't think of Mr Townsend as a twenty year old but rather considered him your equal?'

'In many ways, yes'.

'How did you get on with Mr Townsend's friends? I assume you met them?'

'Yes, of course ... they all seemed very nice'.

'Did you ever go out with Mr Townsend and his friends?'

'No, I preferred not to'.

'Why?'

'Young people have a different idea of fun than somebody my age ... and I don't think any of his friends were as mature as him. Paul behaved differently when he was with his friends ... more their age ... but I guess that's what made him so popular – his ability to adapt'.

'Did Mr Townsend invite you to go out with his friends?'

'Once ... but I think it was purely to be polite ... he wasn't surprised or persistent when I declined and I think he had hoped I'd say no'.

'Did you make any other friends apart from Mr Townsend?'

'I'm friendly with most of the students on my course.'

'As friendly as you were with Mr Townsend?'

'No. There isn't really that much time to socialise ... I'm here to study and there are lots of assignments to do'.

'How many evenings a week would you say you'd spent with Mr Townsend?'

'Three or four, it varied'.

'Did you ever visit Mr Townsend in his accommodation?'

'Yes, several times. We sometimes went back to his college to discuss a lecture or compare notes'.

'And you never thought this might give some people and particularly Mr Townsend himself the wrong impression?'

'No! There were usually other students around ... and whenever we went to his room, the door stayed wide open'.

'Hmm, always? According to other students on the corridor there were times when the door was closed while you were in the room with Mr Townsend'.

'Oh my God! Yes, ok, it happened maybe once or twice that

the door closed accidentally ... and we hadn't noticed until one of his friends knocked on the door to borrow something'.

'And you say you never had a sexual encounter with Mr Townsend?'

'Absolutely not!'

'You spent so much time together and I'm sure sometimes in some very intimate situations and yet, you insist that you never, not even once, felt sexually attracted to Mr Townsend?'

'Never! Oh my God, what is this? Why do you keep on asking me the same thing over and over? I told you, I never considered him in that way and, to my knowledge, neither did he me. I was totally shocked when he suddenly threw himself on me. I thought he'd been drinking before he came ... because his behaviour was different than normal from the moment he'd arrived. But I already told you all that'.

'According to his friends, Mr Townsend told them the night before that he and you had arranged to meet at your house in order to discuss your relationship which he had tried to break off two weeks earlier but was persuaded by your hysterical behaviour to give it another week and then review the situation'.

'What? That's absurd! I don't know who would make up such a story. Which one of his friends told you that lie? I told you, Paul had never been to my house before because I had never invited him and I certainly had not asked him round today ... I wasn't even aware that he knew where I lived ... I was extremely surprised when I opened the door and saw him. At first he said he had visited a friend in the neighbourhood and recognised my car in the driveway but later on he admitted that he'd followed me home one day when I was walking back from the university'.

'Mr Townsend told friends in the common room that he was

worried about meeting you the next day because of your reaction the previous time when he wanted to break up the relationship. We have signed statements from eight people who are all prepared to testify in court'.

'Why would they do this? I understand that they are very upset about Paul's death. So am I! My God so am I. But it was an accident … caused by him … because he was trying to rape me! I don't know what had gotten into him because he had never behaved like this before but he tried to rape me … and as I was fighting him off he fell backwards onto the glass. I am very sad that he is dead but I only defended myself … '

'Mr Townsend had told his friends the night before that you had threatened to accuse him of rape if he tried to break up with you'.

'That's a lie! Break up what? Why won't you believe me?!'

'Please, Mrs Walters, calm down. I believe that you did not kill Mr Townsend with intent but that it was an accident caused by anger and frustration. Break-ups can be very traumatising. You felt humiliated, rejected … '

'Rejected? He tried to rape me! Aren't you listening!?'

'Losing your temper won't solve anything. Now, you might save us both time and yourself a lot of trouble on top if you just tell me the truth about what really happened that day'.

Tiredness and frustration together with everything that had happened in the last few hours was finally getting to Liz and she broke down sobbing, 'I told you the truth … over and over … it happened exactly how I said'.

But the inspector was not taken in by this most common of female defences, 'The evidence suggests otherwise … no matter how much I would like to believe you'.

'My blouse ...', sniffled Liz, 'You saw the state it was in ... he ripped it open, his fingerprints must be on it. Why would he rip open my blouse unless he wanted to rape me?'

'Rather than having been ripped open deliberately, it could have happened accidentally as Mr Townsend was trying to hold on to it in order to prevent himself falling backward when you pushed him. You did push him, yes? You are not denying that?'

'Yes, I did push him', she started to shout, 'I pushed him off me ... because he was trying to rape me!'

'Now, here is where I have difficulties with your statement. Why would Mr Townsend tell all his friends, the day before, that this is exactly what you would be accusing him of the next day?'

'I don't know', she sighed exhaustedly, 'Maybe because it was what he intended to do'.

'You want to tell me that this, in your own words, charming, clever, helpful, popular and handsome young man would maliciously plan to rape a woman who, again in your own words, could have been his grandmother, a woman who was his friend and to whom he had shown nothing but innocent, platonic friendship prior to that day?'

'It's the only explanation I can think of for what's happened'.

'I can think of another explanation: a woman whose young lover was trying to break up the relationship, feels rejected and desperate, is unwilling to accept his plea for freedom, is threatening him with false accusations ... there's a struggle when he is trying to leave, she frantically clings to him, he loosens her grip, she pushes him ...

Liz's upper body slumped onto the inspector's desk, 'No, no, no ....', she cried in total despair.

The next morning, as she was lying there in the dark, too

devastated to sleep, too exhausted to get up, Liz went over and over the recent events. Was Paul really so twisted that he had set up the whole situation? Had he planned to rape her and made up a story for his friends so that Liz's accusations afterwards would lack credibility? Or were Paul's friends, convinced of his innocence, lying in order to avenge his death? Neither scenario seemed plausible. Yet, one was undoubtedly the truth. Which one though? Nobody, apart from her, seemed to care. Her lawyer was confident that she wouldn't be charged with manslaughter as Paul's death was not a direct result of being pushed but caused by accidentally falling on the vodka glass. Had she thrown the glass at him, it would have been a different matter. The police had therefore lost all interest in the case and in her. They didn't care if Liz had a physical relationship with Paul or indeed if Paul was trying to rape her, if he was in fact a psychopath or if his friends were lying to clear their friend's name regardless of whether they believed in his innocence or guilt? So many possibilities, so many question marks and they were all chasing each other in Liz's mind, preventing any restoration of peace.

And, amidst this whirlwind of speculation, every now and then, the disturbed faces of her children popped into her head. They too, didn't care about the truth. They were embarrassed by what had happened, whether she spoke the truth or not. Guilty or not, it did not matter – their mother was somehow involved with a twenty year old kid and that was enough to display signs of revulsion all over their faces. They didn't judge her by what she had done or not, they judged her by how it affected them. Their sole support had consisted of an offer to help with packing up her things. But Liz had no intention of leaving, she was not going to run away, she hadn't done anything wrong. Come what may, she was going to continue to pursue her goal and finish her studies. Even if she had had a sexual relationship with Paul and even if there had been a quarrel just before his fatal accident, she would still not have left now. She was perfectly capable of taking responsibility for her actions which was why she was so disappointed in her children – because they should know that, they should have known that she would hold up her hands – because they had never seen her do anything else. Paul's friends, she could understand why they wouldn't trust her … but her own children?! But she will prove to them that they can always rely on her word and she will put them to shame for doubting her integrity. How dare they look at her with contempt, dismiss her as an embarrassing inconvenience! The more she thought about all the injustice of her situation, the angrier she became. And anger was a good medicine for sorrow, and Liz felt its effect taking over her body and soul. Gone were all signs of fatigue, gone all self pity. By the time she left the house, she did so with her head held high and in fighting spirit.

Liz knew that it would be difficult to return to lectures, to cope with Paul's absence and, indeed, to face Paul's friends … so the sooner she got the first confrontation out of the way, the better. She had some indication of how different life would be for her now the moment she left the house and was rudely ignored by her neighbour who, in the past, had always been extremely friendly . There was no denying that she was nervous when she passed through the faculty gates and it reminded her of the day of her initial arrival here and her first meeting with Paul, and suddenly she was overcome by an uncontrollable sadness as she remembered not Paul, the rapist but, for the first time since his death, Paul, the handsome, clever, witty, confident young man –

her friend, whose loss she had not been able to mourn until now. She felt the tears streaming down her cheeks, unable to stop their flow. She was about to turn around and leave when Malcolm planted himself in front of her, 'You've got a bloody nerve to show your face here!' Next to him appeared Sally, 'Haven't you caused enough damage? Whose life are you going to ruin next?' Then came Peter, Anne, Will, Tim – they all hurled their abuse at her. Which was good, as it dried up her tears because it was exactly what she had been expecting, not grief – the pain of loss was unexpected and had totally overwhelmed her. Now she was back on track, she was ready and determined to receive and survive the blows, 'I know you are upset and I'm terribly sorry ... but none of it is my fault', she said with a sympathetic, yet confident voice while looking from one to the other, meeting each one's eyes. Then she broke through the half circle of hostile youths that had formed in front of her and made her way slowly to the lecture room.

The rest of the day passed quietly. There was lots of staring and whispering but nobody approached her directly. The head of department asked briefly if she was ok, which was nice, otherwise Liz spent her time between the morning and afternoon lecture in the library, popping out only to buy a sandwich. She returned to the library for refuge at the end of the day and didn't leave it until after dark. Determined as she was to be brave and face the repercussions of the past events, she'd had enough for one day and did not want to risk another confrontation. It was unusually warm for mid-May which made her walk home relaxed and pleasant, a stroll rather than the brisk, purposeful walk that gets her from A to B quickly during colder nights. She reflected on the day and, whilst by no means easy, she decided it had been therapeutic. For the first time in days, there were several hours when she had not been tormented by thoughts of what had happened. She had made the right decision by staying. It would have been simpler to leave but the only way to survive emotionally, she was convinced, was to take the complicated route. She was confident that she would get through this and might even discover the truth, she would at least try her utmost. Lost in repeated reassurances that she will prove her innocence, she didn't hear or see them until they had totally surrounded her and then the first blow came so quickly and violently, and the pain took over. At some point, very briefly, she tried to focus on the faces, voices … but couldn't muster enough concentration as she had to give way to the renewed agony that arrived with each blow to every inch of her body. Then suddenly the beatings stopped and for a second Liz thought she had died, but then somebody pulled down her knickers whilst another grabbed her by the hair and she heard this muffled voice close by her ear, 'You want to be raped, do you? Well, now you have a true story to tell.' Then she felt the most excruciating pain of all as something was pushed inside her before she finally lost consciousness.

She vaguely remembered coming round as she was lifted onto a stretcher and put inside the ambulance but other than that, she had no recollection of how she got to hospital nor how and when she was actually found. There was no pain when she awoke but she felt totally immobile, unable even to wriggle her toes. It was quiet and peaceful and she gratefully breathed in the tranquility hoping that it would build up a store of calmness inside her, anticipating that she might need it to draw from when the time came to face the turbulence that so inevitably lay ahead of her.

The door opened and a nurse poked her head round it, 'Good, my love, you are awake, I'll let Doctor Wells know'. A few minutes later a tall, slightly bulky, grey-haired man, probably in his sixties walked in and introduced himself in a loud, bossy, but not unsympathetic, voice, 'I'm Dr Wells, I've patched you up'. Then, whilst looking at the chart, 'No internal injuries, so that's good – a few fractured ribs, fractured nose, concussion, stitching by the lip, stitches by vagina and extensive bruising – so nothing too serious. Having said this, you are lucky to be alive. I hope you are comfortable?' Liz nodded although he clearly didn't expect a response as he carried on, 'We put you on a couple of drips, one of which is a dose of morphine for the pain. I suggest we leave you on that for a few days until your body has mended itself sufficiently to put you on normal painkillers. Otherwise it's plenty of rest and sleep. Oh yes, and I'd advise you to avoid looking in a mirror for the time being – your face is quite swollen and bruised, but I guarantee, none of it is permanent and all should be back to normal in a few weeks. So, that's the physical.

Now emotionally, I would suggest you talk to one of our counsellors. You've just experienced severe trauma, even before the assault and should not underestimate the effect of it.' Liz was about to nod off as it seemed that he'd never stop talking, when she suddenly heard a sharp, 'Any questions?', thrown in her direction. As she tried to speak, she realised the restrictions the stitches imposed to the movement of her mouth, 'You don't want to know what happened?', she mumbled. 'Don't worry', he replied, 'the stitches won't come undone, it'll just feel awkward for a few days. Talking should be fine but be careful with food – steer clear of spare ribs for a couple of weeks!' Liz couldn't bring herself to acknowledge his pathetic attempt of a joke. He was getting on her nerves. He talked too much … and in a tone which indicated zero tolerance for disagreement. Whether Dr Wells noticed Liz's weariness of him or not, he carried on in the same tone, 'And no, I don't need to have further details of what happened – your injuries tell me everything I need to know, the rest is a matter for the police who, by the way, are anxious to talk to you so … whenever you are ready.' Noticing Liz's heavy breathing at his last words, he added, 'I shall refuse them permission until you tell me otherwise'. Liz smiled, relieved and grateful, or at least she'd moved her face muscles to that purpose but could not be sure if her current distortion would translate her intention into a recognisable facial expression. But rather than worrying about it, she closed her eyes and went to sleep.

She woke up with a much clearer head which made her feel able to decide her next step. She knew she had to talk to the police and she intended to do it as soon as possible. But first, she had to be clear whether or not to press charges. Was there any point? She knew exactly who her assailants were but she also knew that it would be impossible to prove their participation. And, forgetting her extreme anger and frustration, it wouldn't solve anything. On the other hand, by not filing charges, it might seem that she is admitting her guilt in Paul's death. One thing, however, she was certain of now – Paul's friends must have been convinced of his innocence! There is no other explanation for the assault on her apart from revenge for their friend's death and their ardent believe in her guilt. And that just confirmed to her that Paul was a twisted young man, a liar, a rapist. He had fooled them all with his good looks, his wit and his charm. But how would she ever be able to prove it?

The two officers who were sent to take down her statement, pulled up a chair either side of her. Liz recognised one of them as the interrogating officer at the initial interview after Paul's death.

The other was a young female and appeared to be of junior rank, taking notes and following her superior's instructions. The young woman who had been introduced to Liz as PC Cooper, asked Liz how she was feeling and pointed out that if Liz felt at any time that she needed a rest, they would stop immediately and commence once Liz had regained her strength. Inspector Brindley was not a man accustomed to wasting time on polite chitchat and after his opening of 'We met before, as you will remember', he immediately hurtled the first question at Liz, 'So why did you remain in Cambridge?' Liz was taken aback. It was a question she had not expected. She had mentally prepared her statement about the attack, gone through carefully who she would name as her abusers, any details of faces, voices, words spoken, various objects she had been able to make out that were used as weapons on her ... but what on earth had her not leaving, not running away got anything to do with the beating she took? Inspector Brindley kept his cold, unemotional eyes on Liz whilst she struggled to overcome her hesitation, 'Erm, erm ... I had done nothing wrong ... I came here to study and ... I could see no reason to abandon my intention to gain a master's degree.'

'So the death of your best friend here did not upset you enough to change your plans?'

Liz, now driven by anger about the repeated injustice, quickly overcame her vulnerability, 'Nor did it have that impact on any of his other friends!' she snapped back. 'As far as I know, nobody left after Paul's death! And what has that got to do with me being violently attacked?!'

'Well, you wouldn't be in hospital right now, would you? I assume you believe you know who your assailants were?'

'I do. You don't want me to tell you what actually happened?'

'PC Cooper will take your full statement later. I'm only interested to see whether there's a case for filing a formal charge against an individual. So, if you would be so kind to just answer my questions as I ask them so that, providing we establish good reason for it, we can start interrogating the suspects. May I point out the importance of acting quickly as the longer we wait, the more time the culprits have to get rid of evidence. So, Mrs Walters, the first name please.'

'Malcolm Rivers, he was Paul's best mate, they've known each other since childhood … grew up …'

'Right, Mr Rivers', interrupted the inspector, 'The relationship between him and the deceased does not matter. Did you see Mr Rivers' face?'

'No'.

'Did you recognise his voice?'

'No, he did not speak … nobody spoke, apart for one person towards the end, just before I lost consciousness … but it wasn't Malcolm'.

'Right', the inspector sighed dismissively, 'Did you see anybody's face?'

'No, they all wore stockings'.

'Did you recognise the voice of the person who spoke?'

'I think it was Peter McLachlan, also a very good … '

'Right', again he cut her short. 'If we get some voice samples, do you think you might be able to identify the voice you heard?'

'I'm not sure … I'll certainly try'.

'Was there anything in particular you noticed … maybe on their clothing? Shoes? Was anybody wearing jewellery? Rings, piercings, tattoos?'

'I think one of them was wearing a ring … not that I saw it …

it just felt as if somebody punched me ... but with something sharper than only a fist ... I have lots of bruises showing a strange pattern ... there are pictures of them somewhere'.

'Yes, we have all the pictures on file already. Did they all hit you with their fists?'

'No, I don't think so ... most of them used a bat of some form. It was too dark to see whether it was a baseball or cricket bat. ... Oh, and I also felt lots of kicking'.

'Nothing significant on clothing then?'

'All I could make out was that they all seemed to be wearing the same thing which looked like these cheap, long plastic rain hoods. It was too dark to make anything out ... also, I guess, at first, I was trying to protect my face and later ... I was only half conscious'. Liz, determined as she was to hold back her tears, couldn't restrain herself any longer and started to cry. 'I remember', she sobbed, 'Trying to make myself focus on their faces .... But the blows came so quickly and the pain ....

PC Cooper intercepted with a calm and sympathetic voice, 'Would you like to rest a little before we continue?'

Liz, fighting hard to regain her composure, sniffled, 'No, it's ok, I'd rather get it over with'.

Showing no compassion for Liz's feelings, Inspector Brindley carried on his questioning in his usual unemotional tone, 'How many would you say attacked you?'

'Five or six. I can't be totally sure ... they had surrounded me and were constantly moving around in a circle ... and they all wore the same raincoat'.

'Did you notice their shoes? Were they light or dark in colour? Did they wear trainers? Any fluorescent stripes maybe?'

'Yes, there was something strange about their shoes – they

were all covered in plastic bags ... the ones which are elasticated on top and are specially made to cover dirty shoes – the ones they use in hospitals ... or gyms. ... Is that of any help?'

'Well, I guess we can rule out a spur-of-the-moment attack. What about height? Was anybody particularly tall or noticeably small?'

'Two were quite a bit smaller than all the others who seemed more less the same height. As far as I know, all of Paul's male friends are quite tall but Sally and Anne are rather petite.

'Are any of the people you named medical students?'

'Clare, Peter and Malcolm. Oh, you think they provided the shoe coverings?'

'Maybe ... but there are other reasons ...', Inspector Brindley suddenly stopped, having decided to keep the thought to himself.

'Is that enough to interrogate anybody?'

'It's enough to ask questions, that's all. So far, we have no real evidence, only suspicions and speculation'. With that, Inspector Brindley got up and, nodding his head in the young officer's direction, he added, 'PC Cooper will now take down your full statement. Should you remember any other detail, no matter how unimportant you might think it to be, make sure you mention it. And, without even a goodbye, he turned round and left. Although already pretty exhausted, Liz managed to finish her statement with PC Cooper.

She woke up to muffled voices and it didn't take her long to recognise them as her children's. She kept her eyes closed, pretending to still be asleep for several more minutes before she felt ready to face them. 'I'm absolutely fine', she chimed in a put-on cheerful tone. 'There was no need for you to come all the way down, you should have just rung.' They both jumped at the sound of her voice and came running to her. They intended to hug her but once close to her bruised face and body, they decided against it, too worried that they might inflict more pain. Sarah started crying, 'Why on earth didn't you leave here?' 'We should have insisted', came Michael's authoritative voice.

'I was never going to run away …. I had no reason to. I've done nothing wrong so why would I abandon my reason for coming here?'

Pointing at Liz's bruises, Sarah was quick to reply, ' To avoid this!'

As always, Michael maintained his calm and rational tone although he agreed with his sister, 'Nobody could have foreseen this … but you should have left nevertheless'.

'Look you two, we are never going to agree on this so let's just drop it. But it's nice to see you both and, although really not necessary, I'm pleased you came. And don't worry, it looks a lot worse than it is … there's no permanent damage and once the swelling subsides and the bruising fades, I'll be as good as new'.

'We know', replied Sarah, 'We spoke to Doctor Wells whilst you were asleep. Such a nice man!'

'Is he?'

'Yes, he is', reassured Michael, 'Haven't you met him yet?'

'I have, but …', Liz hesitated, … 'I found him a little pompous and quite bossy. Well, maybe it was because I saw him shortly after I first woke up'.

'Anyway', continued Michael, 'He told us you'd be ready to leave hospital in a week. We also spoke to Inspector Brindley. So far, it doesn't look if they'll be able to convict anybody as there's no real evidence. He also said that there's absolutely no reason for you to remain in Cambridge.

'I bet he did!', came Liz's indignant reply as she was clearly agitated by Brindley's summary of the case.

'So', Michael tried to conclude, 'Sarah will stay here with you … unfortunately I can't but I'll be back on Saturday by which time you should be well enough to travel. We'll …'

'Stop! Sarah is not staying. You are not coming back. And I'm certainly not leaving!'

'Mum', Sarah chirped in impatiently, 'For God's sake, you can't seriously consider staying!' And, gesturing at Liz's face, she added, 'After all this!'

Michael who had clearly had enough of arguing, decided it was time to put his foot down, 'We won't let you. Not this time … I just wish we had insisted on taking you home a few days ago'.

Liz, realising that she would not succeed in making Sarah and Michael see her point of view, took a deep breath before answering, 'I know you mean well but … it is my decision alone and I've decided to stay until I've finished my Master's'.

'Or until you get killed!', sobbed Sarah.

'Nobody is going to kill me and nobody will harm me again'.

'How can you be so sure?', asked Michael clearly not convinced by his mother's statement. 'Whoever was able to do that to you is capable of doing it again'.

'I really don't think they would. This was the act of a bunch of young misinformed kids who think I had an affair with their friend who then got killed because he tried to break up with me. For some reason, they don't believe the truth – that I never had a sexual relationship with Paul, that he tried to rape me, that I pushed him away in defence and that, by accidentally falling on a glass, cut his artery. If I had left after Paul's death, it would have been like admitting guilt … and the same applies now. I'm telling you, I've done nothing wrong and I shall remain here until I've accomplished what I came here to do. And in the meantime, whilst I'm here, I shall try whatever I can to clear my name. So I would like you both to go home, stop worrying, stop trying to run my life ... and we'll continue to talk on the phone every Saturday as usual'.

'And that's exactly what you would have done', came Michael's frustrated reply, 'if this had happened to one of us, yes?'

'You know that's different', sighed Liz showing signs of fatigue which Sarah was determined to ignore. 'How?', she asked aggressively. 'How is that different? Since we were little, there was a different set of rules – one for us, another one for you! It is time to apply the same rules. We are adults now so if we have no say in matters concerning you then you have no right anymore to interfere in our lives'.

'Sarah, darling, please don't be upset. I know you mean well and I thank you for caring but trust me, I know what I'm doing'.

'Really? Just look at the state of you! And I'm supposed to believe that you know what you are doing?'

'Please, mum', pleaded Michael, 'Let us help you. Come home with us'.

'I can't. I'm sorry if that upsets you ... but the best way to help me, is to support my decision'.

'Support your decision? Huh!' Sarah's voice had jumped an octave higher, 'Like you would support ours in that same situation? You are so selfish, you ...'

'Nor would I doubt that you tell me the truth! Can you say the same? Can you honestly say that you believe that I did not have a sexual relationship with Paul and ...'

'It doesn't matter if you did or not ... we are just pleased that you didn't land in prison!'

Momentarily revived by the anger she felt about Sarah's statement, Liz shouted, 'Because of what? Because I didn't let myself be raped?'

In all her excitement, Liz didn't realise that Dr Wells had entered the room and witnessed the last few minutes of the scene. 'Time out', his booming voice filled the room and Liz immediately fell back onto her propped up pillows exhausted and grateful for his interference. 'Whilst I told you your mother sustained no serious injuries, I don't think she should suffer unnecessary aggravation right now. I suggest you calm down, say goodbye nicely and come back in a few days when she will be almost fully recovered.' He then turned round abruptly and walked to the window where he planted himself, his body language making it quite clear that he would not be the first one to leave this room.

'I see what you mean by bossy', whispered Sarah as she leaned over to say goodbye to her mother.

'I like him more and more', was Michael's comment whilst winking at Liz. Aloud he said, 'Ok, mum, we love you and we do trust you and whatever your decision, we'll support you. For the moment, I believe you are in very good hands so maybe we'll talk in a couple of days.' Sarah, crying again, just managed a sniffling 'Love you, mum' before they both disappeared out of sight.

Her eyes already closed, a barely audible 'Thank you!' was Liz's exhausted response to her rescuer before drifting off into a much needed, albeit short, sleep ... or so it seemed. Not that she didn't feel well rested when she awoke but the fact that Dr Wells was still present and positioned exactly where he was before she had dropped off to sleep, made her suspect that she had nodded off for only a few minutes. Liz felt a little awkward because she wasn't sure if she had fallen asleep whilst Dr Wells had been trying to talk to her but then quickly convinced herself that he, as her doctor, should know that it wasn't rudeness but a condition of the recovery process. 'Children', came his louder than necessary address, 'If they care too little, we are upset and if they care too much, we are even more upset'.

'How many do you have?', inquired Liz purely out of politeness rather than interest.

'Just one – a daughter. Sometimes I don't hear from her for weeks and then she turns up one day and tries to run my life only to disappear again for several weeks when she realises I'm as stubborn as she is. And whilst I'm annoyed about the attempt, I love her for trying!'

Liz tried to laugh but the attempt ended in a grimace due to the restriction caused by the stitches, 'Yeah, I know just how you feel! How old is she?'

'Twenty nine. Since my wife died three years ago, Melanie feels particularly responsible for me … well, every few weeks that is. … What actually happened … erm between you and that young fellow', he asked abruptly. 'The one who died, I mean?'

'As opposed to one of the other young men that I had befriended?' she snapped.

'I don't know how many young friends you had, nor do I care. I'm sorry if my question came out a little clumsily … I just didn't know how to approach the subject'.

'Why would you be interested at all?'

'I've heard various stories about it at the time but I would like to know what actually happened, let's say I have a professional interest'.

'I'll tell you exactly what happened – injustice, that's what happened'.

'Look, I'm not asking out of curiosity … but I might be able to help you … clear your name … that is what you are trying to do, is it not?'

'Trying to … but it's not easy'.

'You were never charged with any wrong doing, is that right? And the case was closed with the young man's death being declared as accidental?'

'Yep! There were no suspicious circumstances regarding the way he died … the dispute was merely whether the preceding argument was because he was trying to rape me or because he was trying to break up with me …'

'And nobody believed your claim that he was trying to rape you?'

'No … his story which he apparently told his friends the night before he died, seemed so much more plausible …'

'Last year, I had a girl in here … she arrived in the early hours of the morning … bruised, beaten and claiming to have been raped by Mr Townsend … She was set on pressing charges so we called the police and she talked to Inspector Brindley but, by the time she left the hospital, she had changed her mind.

''Oh my God! I'm …'

'There's more. A few months ago, another girl came to see us in the middle of the night in a similar state as the first one, making the same claims against Mr Townsend. Again, Inspector Brindley appeared and again, no charges were filed'.

'That bastard! The whole time he treated me like I was the guilty party and Paul was an innocent victim whilst knowing full well that there had been previous accusations of rape! I want to know what Inspector Brindley said to these girls to prevent them from pressing charges and why it would be in his interest to do so?'

'If you could persuade these girls to go public with what Mr Townsend had done to them I don't think anybody would doubt your side of the story. We have records of both cases on our files. And I wouldn't be surprised if you'd discover that there were other girls who decided not to seek medical attention'.

'Why didn't you contact me before?'

'In your case, it was only attempted rape ... and he died trying ... it didn't seem that important and yes, the official story seemed ... erm, well ... plausible. But then I heard you talk to your children and I realised that it is very important that the truth is made public'.

Inspector Brindley arrived within the hour after being summoned by Liz. He flung open the door, knocking only as an afterthought, 'What's the urgency?' Liz had got very to the Inspector's abrupt manner and was only too happy right now to come straight to the point, 'I want to know what prevented you from arresting a rapist when you had two victims willing to bring charges?' If the Inspector was surprised at her question, he certainly did not show it. 'Rape is difficult to prove', came the calm reply.

'Not if the victim checks herself into hospital, beaten up and bruised!'

'It's not as simple as that. These young girls might have been quite willing but didn't like the idea of being a one-night stand'.

'That's the story Paul would have told!'

'Which makes it his word against the girls'.

'Except that both girls had injuries to accompany their story'.

'And Mr Townsend had about twenty witnesses verifying that he came to see them hours before either girl had checked into hospital. On both occasions he seemed calm and collected, with not a scratch on him but aired his concern about the instability of the girl he had just left. Furthermore, with one girl in particular, he seemed to continue to care for days after the alleged assault, telling his friends to be nice to her as she was going through a rough time and claiming that, had he realised that the girl was actually in love with him and looking for a more serious relationship, he would never have slept with her'.

'Yeah, great story! ... Even if you had your doubts the first time, surely, the second time you came across the same allegations you must have at least suspected that there could be some truth in it?'

'Oh, I was convinced the girls weren't lying ... but to prove it was another matter. I had to make clear to the girls what would happen if it goes to court and that there was a chance, due to lack of evidence, that he would not be convicted. Sadly, they both decided not to pursue charges in the end'.

'Because you scared them off!'

'Not me, reality scared them off. I had just been honest with them. Can you imagine what it could do to a young girl? As if rape wasn't enough ... to then expose intimate details in court only to see your assailant walk free! I did however have a private chat with Mr Townsend to make sure he didn't bother these girls any further and to let him know that we'll be watching him. For months no further incidences were reported ... until yours'.

'And all this time, you treated me like a bloody liar!'

'I wasn't aware that I did ... I didn't mean to ... I was frustrated because whilst I wanted to believe your side of the story, there was insubstantial evidence to prove it, which meant Mr Townsend died with his reputation intact ... once again, he got away with it'.

'As his friends will with the assault on me'.

Brindley did not contradict her. Instead, he focused on something that was yet achievable. 'We have one chance left to prove Mr Townsend's guilt – One of the girl's stated that there was somebody else in the room when she was raped. She didn't see who it was … it was too dark but the person didn't seem at all happy about what was happening and kept whispering, 'Stop it Paul, don't be stupid'.

'Do you have any leads to who that person might be?'

'No. Except that it was a he'.

'If the two girls made their experience public, it would give credibility to my account of Paul's attempted rape on me and that I acted in self-defence'.

'Yyees … but it would still not prove it … legally, I mean. We need a conviction otherwise', Inspector Brindley hesitated before blurting out, 'Mr Townsend's parents will file charges of slander and manslaughter against you'.

'What!? How is that possible? I thought the case was closed … declared as accidental death? Which it was'.

'Well, you had pushed him'.

'For good reason! And anyway, as he didn't die as a direct result of my …'

'Their lawyer argues he did. If you hadn't pushed Mr Townsend in the first place, he would not have fallen backwards onto the glass. So, you see, it is very important to prove that you had good cause to push him and that you were acting in self-defence. I can also tell you that the court would not allow any previous rape allegations against Mr Townsend to be brought as evidence.'

'I need to speak to the two girls … and I shall do whatever it takes to find the person who witnessed one of the rapes. I'll even put up fliers and place ads in the local paper … the national papers if I have to, but I shall make him come forward to tell the truth'.

'There are things civilians can do, which the police force can't. All I ask is that you check with me before you embark on anything. We wouldn't want you to do anything illegal'.

Liz, uncertain if the sarcasm was intended or not, answered with a hesitant, 'Right'.

Inspector Brindley, abrupt and unceremoniously as ever, got up and, murmuring a curt 'I'll be in touch', he left.

Liz, by no means anywhere near full recovery, was desperate to get out of hospital and back to uni but Dr Wells refused to sign her release papers before the end of the week and she didn't quite have the courage to discharge herself, which in itself proved that she was indeed not fully fit yet. Her mind however, was working overtime on hatching plans and filing ideas about how to flush out the mysterious witness. First though, she had to find out the names of the two girls Paul had raped in the past. Dr Wells, although firmly set on helping her, was unwilling to breach any doctor/patient confidentiality so she had decided to badger Inspector Brindley to reveal the girls' identities. A task, she anticipated, that would severely challenge her wit and sap all her strength but which, in the end, turned out to be surprisingly easy with the desired information being more less volunteered for the asking. Liz in fact wondered, if only very briefly, how ethical it was to disclose such information and was almost certain that it wasn't. But she had no time now to worry about whether or not Inspector Brindley could get into trouble for it, nor did she intend to reveal her source to anybody.

She was sitting up in bed, quietly listening to her favourite

Beethoven symphony, the Eroica, her thoughts and concentration completely submerged in the little notebook on her lap, that she didn't even notice the door opening and only realised that she had visitors until she heard a shy, soft spoken voice addressing her, 'I'm sorry for disturbing you ... but Inspector Brindley said we should come and see you. I'm Amy and this is Rita'. So that's why Brindley gave up their names without hesitation, 'One mystery solved', thought Liz, he had obviously already known that they were prepared to come forward. Liz invited the girls, who seemed as nervous as they were pretty, to pull up a couple of chairs and sit down. She was determined to put them at ease so she told them that she didn't want to hear any details of what had happened but would like to know whether they'd both be prepared to make a public statement. The girls, appalled by the violent attack on her, promised Liz to do whatever was necessary to finally make public the truth about Paul. Amy, who had clearly still not got over the tremendous emotional trauma she had suffered by the rape and the subsequent injustice that, not only had Paul escaped prosecution but also that he had succeeded in making everybody believe that she was a neurotic, unstable bitch who had made up the rape in revenge because he refused to enter into a relationship with her, remarked bitterly, 'Shame, he won't be alive to suffer some humiliation as the truth about him unfolds'. Rita nodded vehemently in agreement and Liz too, although outwardly not reacting to it, shared Amy's regret. 'We need to find a way of making the person who witnessed Rita's rape come forward. Any ideas?' Rita, who hadn't uttered a syllable so far, shocked them both by saying that she knew who the mystery person is, 'I'm almost certain it was Fred. I even spoke to him about it at the time, shortly after leaving the hospital. He denied it of course, saying he hadn't seen Paul that night and only ran into him at breakfast the next morning. I could tell he was lying because he felt uncomfortable and he never questioned that the rape took place, nor did he ever join in with the others when they accused me of inventing the rape.

'Did you not mention his name to Inspector Brindley at the time?'

'There was no point, Fred was not going to budge ... he had already sorted out an alibi by the time I talked to him – apparently he'd hung out with Matt, his room mate, all night'.

' Did nobody on your corridor hear anything that night? I mean there must have been a lot of noise when you were trying to fight him off?'

' No, there was a big party two floors down ... he picked the perfect night'.

'It was the same with me', said Amy, 'Everybody was out that night clubbing because it was the twin's 21st. The bastard had really planned ahead!'

'I think the three of us should talk to Fred together', suggested Liz, 'Maybe even involve Inspector Brindley ...'

Rita shook her head, 'Let me try on my own again'.

'Why would you think he'd tell you more this time?'

'Firstly, because Paul is dead – I think that makes a difference ... and then, erm', Rita blushed and continued slightly embarrassed, 'I know that Fred has a crush on me ... so, that might help'.

Liz smiled, 'It might. Anyway, thank you both. I am so grateful that you've decided to come forward and I don't want to rush you but ... Paul's parents have filed charges against me for manslaughter and slander'.

'We know', said Amy, 'Inspector Brindley told us'.

Rita looked at her watch, 'I've arranged to meet Fred in an hour'.

'Thank you', sighed Liz letting her head drop back onto the propped up pillow.

'Well, it's not just for your benefit', declared Rita, 'Amy and I have spent months trying to find a way of exposing him … but whilst he was with you he didn't show much interest in anybody else and we thought that he had finally found somebody who made him happy … it never occurred to us that you were his next target'.

'I never had a sexual relationship with him … and I can assure you I never felt that way about him … nor did it ever enter my mind that he should think of me like that. Of course I found it weird at first that he should seek my company but then I thought that maybe he needed a mother figure in his life … and we did get on very well … anyway, he deceived lots of people with his charm'.

'I just feel', added Amy with tears in her eyes, 'That unless it's all out in the open, I won't be able to move on with my life … I've already lost a lot of time. I don't even know anymore what was worse – the actual rape or the continuous public humiliation because people believed I had made it all up'.

The girls kept their promise. A few days later, Dr Wells brought Liz the Cambridge Gazette and there on the front page with the headline *"The Talented Mr Townsend"* was an article about Amy, Rita and Fred revealing the truth about Paul Townsend. Also mentioned was the attempted rape on Liz Walters whose self-defence had led to the young man's accidental death.

FROM LOVE TO HATE – IN TEN SECONDS

Julia signed the divorce papers without hesitation. No regrets. She didn't care who got the house, the shares, the orchard – she just wanted Chris out of her life. She put the papers in the envelope. She will have them biked over to Chris immediately, hoping that he would sign them straight away. She felt nothing but relief. No matter how long and hard she thought of her fifteen year marriage, she could not recall the love she once felt for Chris – only the moment she started to hate him.

It had been such a peaceful morning! Chris had taken Michael to school so she was able to have a relaxed breakfast, reading the paper whilst savouring several cups of hot coffee – a true luxury compared to the cold half cup she normally managed to gulp down before running out the door. On top of that, Michael was going to a birthday party after school and was then spending the night at a friend's house which meant she had the whole day to herself! No school run, no cooking! She could have her shower and get ready whenever she liked and then drive into town at leisure to meet Chris at 5.30 for a pre-theatre dinner.

She remembered leaving the house that day, feeling like a new person. For the first time in weeks she liked what she saw in the mirror – a well groomed, reasonably attractive woman! She'd left in plenty of time, not wanting to spoil the calmness of the day with a frantic car journey. Driving along Kingsfield Road, she was pleasantly surprised that there wasn't much traffic, allowing the cars to drive at the set 30 mph speed limit rather than crawling along at 20 mph or less during rush hour, which she had to suffer through on her daily school run.

Arriving at the restaurant half an hour early, she treated herself to a glass of Prosecco whilst reading her texts, one from

Chris saying he'd try and get there a bit earlier too. Dinner had been great, the play, Richard III, was fantastic with some exceptional performances. They both agreed they had to do this more often. Shame though that they had to go back to Chris's office afterwards to pick up his car as he needed it in the morning. She thought at the time that it was silly having to drive back in two cars. She had assumed he would leave his car in the office car park overnight. Had she known that he needed his car the next morning to drive to an out-of-town meeting, she would have taken the train in. Definitely. He should have told her. She still couldn't understand why he hadn't.

Chris loved his Porsche. It was his answer to his mid-life crisis. And he liked showing it off, which had resulted in a few speeding tickets. So of course she was not surprised when he sped past her at the first opportunity on the way home that night. She hadn't minded. And she hadn't lagged behind too far, after all her Mercedes was a sports one and quite capable of keeping up the speed.

Prior to that day, she had always loved driving at night when there was hardly any traffic. But that too had changed, like so many things since then. She had noticed the group of people in the distance and had started screaming the moment she saw the boy running out into the road because she knew that Chris would not be able to stop in time. She had heard the thump, had seen the tiny body somersaulting through the air. She had slammed her foot on the brakes and jumped out of her car, ran past Chris who was standing there like an idiot crying, 'You've seen it, you must have seen it, he just ran out, there was nothing I could do, you ...' She did not hear, did not care what he was saying because it did not matter. He didn't matter. Nothing mattered anymore ... and never

ever would again. 'Michael, Michael!' was all she had managed to shout, over and over and over … but nothing could bring her son back to life.

A GOOD DEAL

Sitting at the kitchen table, Edward was staring at the heap of paperwork in front of him. He was sick of the sight of unpaid bills, demands from creditors, threatening letters from his bank. He knew there was a limit to how long he could ignore them, and it was close. There was however one item of post that morning which could not be ignored. He placed the unfolded document on the table but separate from the rest of the pile to make sure his wife would see it when she came downstairs. This way, by discovering it herself, he would not be the bearer of the bad news and she might not direct her anger and frustration at him.

When, a few minutes later Sarah emerged, she gasped in shock at the sight of the court order and collapsed into a chair sobbing, 'How long have you known?' Edward expected her to be devastated but he was also aware that they urgently had to find somewhere else to live, and he needed Sarah to stop feeling sorry for herself and focus on what had to be done. It could hardly have come as a surprise to her. 'For sure', he answered calmly, 'Only this morning, but I was expecting it for some time. We have to go through our options'.

'What options?' she shouted hysterically, 'We have no bloody options left! Don't make it sound as if we had a choice.'

'I've registered for a council ….'

'Stop!' she screamed covering up her ears, 'I don't want to hear it!'

Sarah's initial approach to any crisis had always been denial, followed by diverting her rage and resentment to blaming somebody, mostly her husband, for the problem. Edward, so used to Sarah's irrational behaviour when it came to dealing with realities she didn't like, was desperately trying to avoid an argument so he continued in a gentle tone in the hope to soften the blow when introducing the next topic – their daughter. So far, they had managed to keep their financial disaster from their daughter which, although not always easy, had been possible because Helen was attending a boarding school and only came home during holidays. So, with a few lies regarding some facts concerning their current accommodation as being an interim solution whilst they were trying to look for a new house, plus various other fibs to explain the lack of cash, Edward and Sarah had made sure that Helen was oblivious to their mounting problems. And one thing both parents had always agreed on was not to upset their daughter unnecessarily. However, the time had come when Helen had to be confronted with the truth about their situation. 'We have to think of how and when to tell Helen', stated Edward as composed as possible.

'No!' shouted Sarah frantically' 'I cannot bear it! 'She doesn't need to know … not yet!'

But Edward handed her another letter explaining, 'Unless we pay the school fees for the whole year by the end of the month, they won't let her come back after half term'.

Sarah had firmly believed in the school's loyalty and support and had been convinced that Hawthorn would keep Helen on, despite their financial difficulties. To find now that this was not the case drove Sarah into a total frenzy. 'They can't do that!', she howled and wept, 'They can't just abandon her. She is one of their brightest students. Last term, she was top again in maths. They can't just not care!'

'Sarah', Edward tried to appease her, 'They are running a business, not a charity, regardless of what they claim. They have other talented students whose parents can pay the bills. And, as they say', he added sarcastically, 'Helen is a very bright girl who will do well wherever she goes. Fair or not, Sarah, we have to talk to Helen now because we have to move out of here in ten days and half term starts in a couple of weeks'.

But as always, Sarah convinced Edward to postpone telling Helen, arguing that it would be better to keep the truth from their daughter until her return from boarding school at half term, as this way Helen would not have to cope with the disastrous news whilst still at Hawthorn. Sarah's procrastination was not just cowardice, it was also due to being an eternal optimist. As long as there was hope, she would not be defeated. And it was because she possessed this fighting spirit that she often got upset with Edward, who had always so readily accepted everything. Whilst she clung to some shred of hope that their situation might yet change, that her husband might yet find another job, Edward had accepted that they were destitute. At sixty-one, he knew very well that nothing but a miracle could save them from bankruptcy. Sarah accused Edward of being unduly relaxed for their circumstances and of not caring enough, to which he responded that she was confusing keeping a clear head and dealing with the situation with being laid back. 'We can't both be running around like headless chickens', he scolded her. 'The difference between you and me', she snapped back, 'is that I won't stop fighting until the end whilst you always capitulate without a fight.'

'What you call fighting is just stubbornness – a childish unwillingness to accept an unavoidable situation'.

'That's your answer to everything, isn't it? We must accept reality. Has it ever occurred to you that we can change reality? If you got a job, our reality would be different, wouldn't it?'

Despite his best intention to avoid an argument, Sarah always found a way to get to him. 'You are a real bitch sometimes', he finally exploded. 'Who insisted on taking out a loan to keep Helen in private education? Who had to spend £500 on a birthday party for Helen when we were already struggling to pay the rent? Who is responsible for the fact that our credit card bills are used up to their maximum?'

'Ok', Sarah admitted, 'I found it difficult to cut back at first but so did you! I wasn't the only one spending money we didn't have! Don't you dare and try and blame that whole mess on me! But you know what really infuriates me? That you are so bloody unaffected when our lives are about to be destroyed!'

These quarrels, like most arguments, never solved anything and served no other purpose but to let off steam. And what did it really matter how and why they ended up in such dire straits, or indeed whose fault it was?

Plagued by worries, Edward could not sleep properly that night. He had nodded off a few times but mostly he was just tossing and turning until he eventually decided to go downstairs to get a cup of tea.. There, in the dimly lit kitchen, he found a man sitting at the kitchen table. Despite the strangeness of the situation, Edward did not act surprised. 'What do you want?', he placidly asked the stranger. 'To help you', came the visitor's cheerful reply.

'Really?', Edward smirked and continued sarcastically, 'So you are going to give me two million pounds?'

'If that's what it takes', replied the Man nonchalantly.

'And why would you do that?'

'To help you.'

'So you are just going to hand over £2 million pounds? Just like that, huh?'

'Well, I thought I'd offer you a deal.'

'What sort of deal?'

'A good deal. You have something I want and I offer £2,000.000 for it.'

'I have nothing left of any value, look around you. ... I can offer you my services.'

The Man looked Edward up and down, then replied slowly, 'No, thank you.'

Edward, realising the misunderstanding, replied quickly, 'I didn't mean personal services.' Then added jokingly, 'But for £2 million, I guess ...' He gave a little chuckle before continuing in a grave voice, 'Well, that's really all I'd have to offer you ... my body and my soul! And I'd gladly give you both', he finished slightly pompously.

The Man laughed out loud, 'Your soul is worthless!'

'Sorry', replied Edward apologetically, 'I don't believe in that nonsense either ... just a manner of speech. Seriously though', he continued with sternness and determination in his voice, 'I would give my life!'

'You think your life is worth more than your soul?' The Man seemed surprised.

'Soul, eternal life – pah, all make-believe. We have to live while we can and make the most of it. Carpe diem! That's always been my motto – grab it while you can!'

A flicker of a smile appeared on the Man's face as he replied barely audibly, 'Carpe anima (seize the soul)! That's mine – grab them while they are pure!'

Edward assured the Man that if his family were to benefit from his death, he would not hesitate to even take his own life, right now. But what seemed like a heroic statement to Edward, was instantly dismissed by the Man as meaningless and he pointed out that, regardless if dead or alive, neither Edward's body nor soul held any worth. But, the Man insisted, 'You have one thing that's very valuable'. Edward, knowing very well that he had sold everything that was worth anything, replied confidently, 'Well, whatever you think it is, you are welcome to it'.

'You have a daughter ... young and pure ... with a soul like an angel'.

Edward was shocked, appalled, 'You're after my daughter? You must be mad if you think I'd sell my daughter!', he exclaimed indignantly, 'She's 14 years old! You pervert! You paedophile!'

Realising that Edward had jumped to the wrong conclusion, the Man quickly replied, 'Whoa, whoa! I'm not interested in her body, you misunderstood. I merely want her soul and for that I offer you two million pounds'.

'Her soul?' asked Edward in disbelief. 'I told you I don't believe in this soul business ... and even if I did, it wouldn't be mine to give'. But the Man assured him that because Helen was a minor, he could not approach her directly and it was therefore her guardians' decision. 'So, how about it? Your daughter's soul in exchange for two million pounds? As you don't believe in everlasting souls', he added, 'What prevents you from promising it to me? Seems you have nothing to lose.'

Edward, instead of being delighted and immediately accepting the stranger's offer, hesitated. He was not a religious man and did not want to take advantage of somebody who clearly was a believer. 'It would be wrong', he therefore declined, 'I feel I would rob you of your money.'

'I wouldn't worry', the Man comforted him. 'It is a truly good deal when both parties believe they get a bargain!'

Edward wasn't sure if he was dreaming or not because it all seemed so real and yet it couldn't be. Suddenly, he heard Sarah's shrill voice, 'Of course we'll do it! For goodness' sake, Edward, what's there to think about?!' Unbeknown to Edward, Sarah had been standing outside the kitchen door, listening to the whole conversation. He stared at his wife 'So it's not a dream?', he asked in amazement. 'No', Sarah reassured him, 'God is giving us a last chance. The Man is right, it's a good deal!' For Sarah, who did not believe in God either, the Man's offer seemed perfect. As far as she was concerned, they could only win. She urged her husband to see sense but something didn't seem right to Edward. 'How would this deal affect Helen?', he asked suspiciously.

'You mean apart from never finding out how close she was to leading a miserable life?', came the Man's agitated answer.

'Helen would not know about our deal?', Edward persisted on questioning the Man.

'Not whilst she is alive.'

'You promise Helen will be happy as long as she lives?'

'Blissfully.'

'You swear you won't contact Helen and try and seduce her?'

'If that's all you are worried about', laughed the Man, 'then rest assured'.

'What other worries should I have', asked Edward somewhat alarmed.

'None', replied the Man coldly, 'as you don't believe in the human soul'.

'Swear!', demanded Edward, 'That Helen will lead a happy life.'

'I swear', the Man obliged in a bored tone, 'by all the innocent souls still left on this earth, that your daughter will be as happy as can be for as long as she lives.'

'Your obsession with souls!', cried Edward. 'You must swear by something I believe in.'

'Alright', sighed the Man, 'I swear by all the money in the world!' He was clearly starting to become impatient. 'So, do you want to save your daughter from the harsh reality; from losing her friends; from poverty; from a future paved with problems and uncertainty; ... from discovering all your lies? Two million pounds would solve all your problems – school fees, new house, car ... but if you'd rather tell your daughter that, from one minute to the next, her life will change from luxury to the abyss, then ...

'No!', screamed Sarah in horror. 'We'll do it. Let's do it now!'

'Sarah', interrupted Edward, 'Your reaction is purely Machiavellian. But the end doesn't always justify the means – sometimes it's worth to adjust the outcome in order to keep the means dignified. So let's think about it for a moment. The man is offering us a lot of money for ... nothing ... a myth. It would be immoral to accept.'

'Morals!', screeched Sarah, 'You can't afford them!' This is our last chance, not taking it would be unforgiving. Could you seriously look at Helen confronting her with our miserable fate knowing that you didn't do everything possible to avoid it? How would Helen feel if she found out that we had an opportunity to give her a wonderful life but you decided not to take it.'

'At least we have to try to be honest.' Edward turned to the Man, 'I would like to tell you the truth.'

'About what?' asked the Man puzzled.

'Souls'.

'I know the truth about souls.'

'You see, Edward', whispered Sarah, 'The Man knows what he is doing. It's not that we intend to cheat him – and remember, he approached us, he came to us. I swear to God, Edward, if we don't make this deal, I shall leave you and make sure that you'll never see Helen again!'

'I give up', said Edward as he, finally defeated, nodded in agreement, 'Ok, go ahead.'

Sarah, now beaming, turned to the Man who assured her that, as long as their decision was unanimous, no contract was needed to seal the deal, no handshake necessary. He then promised that in a few days they would receive a cheque for two million pounds from a company called 'Marlboro Insurance'.

The next day, neither Edward nor Sarah were too sure if the events of the previous night had been a dream or not. Yes, it seemed weird that they should both have had the same dream, but weirder still that somebody should just hand over two million pounds without getting anything in return. Sarah wanted it to be real with all her heart but even she had doubts. The Man did not re-appear on any subsequent night and, when three days later still no cheque had arrived, Edward reminded Sarah that it was time to face reality. 'Come on, darling', he nudged her, 'We need to start packing things up.'

'It might arrive yet', she said, sounding none too convinced herself. ' He did say a few days. Oh, Edward, I wanted so much for it to be real, I was ready to believe anything that gave me hope. But I guess, it was too good a deal.

'I know', Edward replied sympathetically, 'But now let's get on with it.'

They had just started the painful task of wrapping up some framed photographs – a reminder of happier days, when they heard the post being delivered. Sarah, as she had done these last three days, immediately ran to the door. Edward was still shaking his head at his wife's unfaltering optimism, when he heard her screaming, 'It's here, it's here!' Sarah came running into the kitchen and, against all expectations, held up a cheque for two million pounds! Edward and Sarah were delirious with joy. And after they had exhausted themselves with jumping and dancing around, they started to discuss what to buy first – a car, a house, clothes. 'Whoever says that money can't buy happiness', Sarah chirped, 'Is a great big liar.'

When half an hour later the doorbell rang they both went to answer it. They were ready to face anything now – more bills, angry creditors, a livid landlord – there was nothing they couldn't cope with. As the two stern looking police constables asked to be let in, Sarah and Edward just smiled at each other confident in the knowledge that their newly acquired wealth would sort out everything.

'I'm terribly sorry', one of the policeman said gravely, 'but there's been an accident. Your daughter was involved in a car crash during a school outing. Sadly, neither she nor the driver of the car survived. I am so sorry. Your daughter's school and the driver's insurance company will be contacting you shortly.'

Sarah was too shocked to accept what she had just heard, 'It can't be true', she insisted, 'There must be a mistake'. Edward sank into a chair as the realisation of what had happened, of what they had done, became clear to him, 'And the driver's insurance company', he almost choked as he spoke, '... is Marlboro Insurance?' He didn't need to hear the answer to know he was right.

JUST IN CASE

The moment Harry had closed the front door, he took the letter which he had so far stubbornly refused to read, out of the inside pocket of his jacket and put it on the kitchen table. Armed with an ice cold beer, he sat down, tore open the sealed letter and started to read

Just in case...
... if you want to use our car, the keys are in the tray on the piano – should you lose them, there's a spare set in the garage (blue and white chest of drawers, top drawer, underneath the small box of nails and screws). But drive carefully! And remember, it's a much faster car than you are used to. And don't drink and drive – ever!! Even if you only had one drink and you feel ok, don't do it, it's just not worth it. Remember this case (it was in the papers) a few years ago when this eighteen year old boy caused an accident whilst over the limit and, although nobody was injured, because he ended up with a drink-driving conviction, Cambridge University withdrew their offer of a place! Isn't that awful? You could ruin your whole future – just consider that! You shouldn't need to put any petrol in for a while (you know dad likes to have at least half a tank full at all times!) but should you need to top it up or if you need any cash for any other reason, there are a hundred pounds in the middle drawer of the bookshelves in the living room.

Should you ever lock yourself out, our neighbour has a key. So don't panic if you do, it's really nothing to worry about – these things happen. When I was your age, I managed to lock myself out a few times – it's a teenager's prerogative to be spaced out and forgetful. Besides, you always had a strange relationship with keys. Remember when you were about four years old and you hid the keys under the piano, behind one of the legs? I was going mad because I was convinced that I had left the keys in the front door lock on the outside and somebody walking past had taken them. You and I were leaving that same evening to go away for a week, leaving dad on his own. I made dad promise that he'd have all the locks changed first thing in the morning. When later, on the plane, you whispered to me that you knew where the keys were, I did not believe you. But when I rang dad, I asked him to check under the piano where you had claimed to have put them, just in case. We couldn't believe that you hadn't said anything sooner! We often laughed about it later, not at the time though. Can you imagine, we almost had all the locks – windows, security gates, the lot – changed! And then there was that time when you fished the house keys out of dad's jacket pocket whilst we were having dinner at the Italian restaurant round the corner (although your three friends who came to stay the night may have had something to do with it). When we got home, you let dad run back to the restaurant to search for his keys before you showed them to me. Of course, you and your pals thought this was hilarious but it wasn't easy to calm dad down and you were very lucky that you were still allowed to watch a movie that evening! You were such a rascal! But we wouldn't have wanted you any other way!

I knew you were a cheeky little so and so the moment you were born – the first time you opened your eyes, I noticed that little twinkle, which you still have by the way, that promised you'd keep us on our toes. But you are also the most affectionate and in many ways, the most perfect son we could ever have wished for. You have achieved so much already because whenever you decided to do something, you gave it one hundred percent! I hope you never lose that focus and determination. You never disappointed us. Not that this would be possible – we love you far too much – but you always managed to top our expectations and hopes, academically as well as with your sporting achievements. I'll never forget, when you were not quite five years old, you came home from school and said you needed to revise for your (first ever!) school exams. I laughed (I'm so sorry) and told you not to be so silly because I considered you far too young to take exams seriously– you came second overall (but were first in maths, English and science)! From then onwards, I did not stop you from revising and you came first in every subsequent exam for the next several years. And yet, you never revised as much as some of your peers. Even in later years, I never saw you stressed out over homework or exams like many other boys in your school but you still managed two scholarships and five fantastic A levels! You are very gifted – never lose sight of that – and you have the potential of being very successful.

At prep school, one of your form teacher's comments was that 'whilst shy at times, you often displayed strong leadership qualities' – a perfect combination! I knew exactly what she was talking about! When you were twelve, just a couple of months before sitting the scholarship exam for the best senior school in the country, we had decided to move and therefore the property was being shown frequently. One of the Estate Agents had a habit of turning up unannounced which infuriated me and once, you had just come home from playing rugby and where all caked up with mud, I intended to quickly pop out to the shops whilst you had your shower. Just as I was about to open the front door, the bloody estate agent unlocked the door and wanted to show the place – again without appointment or prior warning. I told her she couldn't come in as I had to go out and you were on your own, about to have a shower. She was very persistent and didn't want to take no for an answer. I was about to say no for the third time when you suddenly came pounding down the stairs, still filthy and in your rugby gear and said in a very authoritative voice: "Didn't you hear, she said no." The woman looked at you and all she managed to reply was: "Sorry, Sir" and she was gone. I was so impressed with the way you had taken control and so proud of you!

And you are so handsome as well! It'll be difficult to fend off all these girl! I know you are not gay, not that we would have loved you less if you were ... well, I wouldn't anyway, dad's a bit funny in that respect but I'm sure he'd have come round if you had been. No, I realised you were into girls when I found the pictures hidden (not well enough though!) under your mattress. Don't be embarrassed, it's natural, a healthy curiosity is part of the normal process of growing up. Dad was so proud of you when I showed him the pictures – more so, I think, than when you got your first scholarship! Silly Man!

You must ring Auntie Mary – she'd love to hear from

you and she'll be able to help you with anything you might need. I also enclose another list of phone numbers and addresses that might be useful, like our plumber's number, for instance. You can call Keith any time, day or night, he is extremely nice and he will come out in the middle of the night in an emergency and without charging a horrendous call-out fee! (Obviously, don't call him at two in the morning for a dripping tap).

Make sure you lock the patio door at night. It's a bit temperamental at times but you just need to pull it quite hard towards you and then it should be ok (it's because the wood warps due to the temperature changes).

You need to get the cat from the cattery. We paid up to Saturday so if you collect him later than that, you'll have to pay the difference. Remember, he only eats dry food and he needs fresh water every day (make sure he always has water in his bowl). And keep the bedroom doors closed otherwise he'll lie on the beds and you'll end up with cat's hair everywhere (he seems to be losing more fur than ever at the moment, I'm surprised he isn't bald yet). If you feel like it, you could brush him every now and then – he loves it and it helps a bit to control the hair shedding (his brush is in the cupboard underneath the sink). Don't use the metal side of the brush, he hates that and might bite you – only use the bristle side. Otherwise he is no problem at all. He hardly goes out at all these days (too old, I guess) but he'll let you know when he wants to. Of course, you'll have to clear out his litter tray every morning. And if you need fresh litter, there's a new pack in the garage next to the freezer.

Rubbish collection is every Monday for normal household

waste and food disposal and every Wednesday for paper, plastic and glass. Try and separate your rubbish otherwise the bin will get too full too quickly and the lid won't fit properly which would be an invitation to all the foxes! You know we have lots of foxes in the neighbourhood and they'd just create havoc. You'd have all the rubbish scattered outside the front door!

All information and contact details regarding any household appliances including television, phone and broadband are in a file marked "household info" which is in the hall cupboard, right hand side, bottom shelf. Bank details and other essential phone numbers and contact details are on the attached list.

I bought you a few clothes (your favourite brand) in the sale and they are hanging up in your room, the receipt is on your desk, just in case you need to return anything. Providing it all fits, I think you'll like everything –apart from, maybe the jacket, it might be a bit bright for you. You always disliked bright colours, particularly bright green for some reason, and preferred blue, black and brown. I shall never forget when you were three, I bought you a bright, grass green jacket (it was gorgeous and very expensive) to replace your by then shabby looking, navy jacket which you had outgrown. Having disposed of the old one, I simply put the new coat on your hook in the hall to surprise you with it the next morning. Well, the surprise was all mine! You cried and screamed that this was not your coat, therefore you would not wear it and you wanted **your** coat back! After a battle which lasted over an hour, we finally left the house with you wearing your brand new coat – you were eventually persuaded when I told you that the Easter Bunny had brought you this new jacket and taken the old one away and if you didn't wear it, you would upset the Easter Bunny and he might not return on Easter Sunday. I did win that one, but I had learnt my lesson – I never surprised you with any bright clothing again! (Until now!)

You were always very sporty – tennis, football, rugby, cricket, you did it all. And Dad was the one who would go and watch every game you ever played in – he was a permanent fixture on the side line! I must admit, I was surprised when you first mentioned, aged five, that you wanted to join the school's football club but dad was delighted and it became apparent very quickly that you were quite good. We shall never forget your first football match against another school when you could only play the first half because we had booked to go to Paris that day. We had a taxi waiting to take us to Eurostar and basically had to drag you off the pitch, but only after you had scored the winning (and only) goal of the match! Similarly, you shocked me when you were desperate to start rugby although looking at some of the pictures when you were little, those sturdy legs should have given me a hint! Your first rugby match, in your first scrum (I think that's what it's called) you ended up on the floor and somebody stepped on your head, accidentally I'm sure because nobody actually knew what they were doing at that age. You were lying there for a couple of minutes, clearly in pain so we asked the coach if you should maybe come off but by the time he turned to look at you, you had already jumped up and were running after the ball. Your coach looked at dad and said:

well, there's your answer. It was obvious that you loved the game and we were so proud of you, particularly dad – his son, clever, handsome and sporty! He was beaming for the rest of the day. Sorry, this sounds as if we wouldn't have loved you as much or been as proud of you were you lacking any of these traits. You must never believe that. When you were born, we were ready to accept and love you unconditionally. And whatever your achievements, they are ultimately for your benefit alone even though it may not always have seemed that way when you were little as of course, you wanted to please us and were looking for our approval. And I'm sure you had doubts about the positive effects on your future every time I tore up a piece of homework when it was of inferior standard to what you were able to produce. Ok, it didn't happen too often but every now and then you'd get so lazy! Once, I think you were about eight or nine, you wrote an essay which was really good apart from the last sentence when you'd obviously decided that you'd had enough so you finished with "and then we went home" – now, I couldn't possibly let you hand that in – you would have never made the scholarship class!

Dad just reminded me that I'm supposed to write a note just in case, not a book. He says, the most important thing you need to know, apart from the info on the enclosed contact list, is that we love you. And he wants you to keep on supporting Chelsea regardless of their performance! He is of course right but, for some reason, I keep getting carried away. I should be packing by now and be looking forward to our cruise and three weeks of sunshine. And I do, and I know that nothing is going to happen to us – but then I think well, just in case something does happen …

Actually, reminiscing with a pen in my hand is not a bad thing as you won't remember much of your first few years (and certainly nothing from when you were a baby) and nobody knows any of this apart from dad and me because we never had any relatives living near us so, just in case …

You were born on a Thursday, at five to eleven at night, weighing a whopping ten pounds and they had to use forceps to deliver you. Even the doctor who delivered you was surprised by your size. I was in labour for about thirteen hours and dad was present at your birth. We returned home the next day but a few days later you were diagnosed with jaundice and we had to go back into hospital for another three days during which time you were placed in an incubator and I could only take you out and hold you for feeding. It was one of the most difficult times of my life. Sometimes you were lying in there crying and all I could do was put a finger on your little hand through a small opening on the side of the incubator – so whilst you screamed pitifully inside your tiny glass box, I was sobbing away outside. It was so hard but I was told that the more I took you out, the longer it would take for the jaundice to subside. Still, we made up for it when we returned home! For the first few months, you slept in our bed all night because whilst I was breastfeeding you, we'd often both fall asleep and feeding you during the night was so much more convenient when you were lying right next to me. And you were a very hungry little boy who needed a lot more food than I first realised. But because of that, you also grew very quickly. The first time I took you for a check up to the baby clinic, I was given a little booklet to record your progress, immunisations etc. (we've still got it, it's on the middle shelf in the hall cupboard in a file named 'medical') On the first page, there is a printed growth chart, indicating the lowest guideline in blue and then about an inch up a black line for the highest. You will notice a red line about half an inch up from the black one – that was your unique growth line which they had to draw in specially as you did not fit the norm!

But I only truly realised how much food you needed once I started you on formula milk. I first gave you one bottle and when you were still crying after you had finished it, I thought you suffered from wind and it took a while before I realised you were still hungry but I couldn't understand why you were still crying after the second bottle! Well, it took three bottles a night before you were content and went to sleep. Once I had recognised your desperation to grow and the amount of food necessary for your needs, you were a perfectly happy baby – as long as I made sure you were properly fed, in clean nappies and had peace and quiet when you wanted to sleep. However, failure to provide any of this, would most definitely end in disaster as you were persistent and always very demonstrative – you would not stop screaming until your requirements were fulfilled. Sociable as you were when awake and smiling at everybody but when you decided it was time to sleep, I had to take you somewhere quiet, if it so happened that we were in a restaurant, I had to take you outside to make sure you weren't disturbed by the chattering of fellow diners. Once asleep, I could bring you back inside and you would sleep peacefully without being bothered by any surrounding noise.

You always took the same determined approach to anything you had decided to do. Even potty training! Actually, you never used a potty – you went straight from nappies to using a proper loo, albeit with a child seat on top. We tried you on a potty but, maybe because you were quite big, you hated squatting so low down. (Or maybe it was that your pudgy little rugby legs wouldn't bend properly!) But once you discovered the toilet, there was no turning back. I remember taking you for a picnic and putting a nappy on you, just in case. By the time I had unpacked all the food, you announced that you had to do a pooh. I told you it was ok to do it in the nappy because I was prepared and had brought nappy sacks, wipes and a fresh nappy but you wouldn't hear of it. I suggested the nearby bushes but to no avail – I had to pack everything up and take you home! You also went through a long phase, lasting several years, when you refused to use any public toilet and I'm probably responsible for that – sorry – as I've always made such a fuss about not touching anything and spending ages securing the seat with tissue paper. When you were about five or six, I was out shopping one day when I received a phone call from your headmistress at school saying you were very unwell and complaining of a severe headache so could I get you as soon as possible. Of course, I dropped all the shopping and went to collect you. One look at you and I knew what was wrong – you were desperate to go to the loo and there was no way you'd go at school! Mind you, you were not the only one. Comparing notes with some of your friends' mothers at the time, you all suffered the same phobia.

As a baby, you loved being naked and therefore really enjoyed nappy changing time because I would often leave you lying there for a while without a nappy, tickling you and letting you kick your legs. Of course, and it had to happen one day, I left the nappy off for just a bit too long – yes, you peed right into my face, giggling all the way! Dad, who was watching, thought it was hilarious.

You were two and a half when you started nursery but it took you a while to settle in. The first few days, the moment I arrived back home after dropping you off, I'd get a phone call from the nursery asking me to please collect you as you would not stop screaming. After a week, I decided to just wait outside in the car for half an hour! A few weeks later though you loved it there and you made some nice friends who ended up in the same pre-prep school as you.

You had your collar bone fractured twice – the second time, which you will remember, was whilst playing rugby, the first time was when you were four and a half whilst at home fooling around with some friends after school. It was your first term at pre-prep and your form teacher had every boy in your class make you a card (I kept them, they are in one of the wooden boxes in the garage). You only stayed at home for a week and then insisted on going back to school wearing your arm in a sling and were not allowed to write for at least two weeks. You received your first form prize that year. The little scar by your eye is from when you were messing around whilst brushing your teeth, aged two, and you fell off the little stool (which you needed to reach the washbasin) and hit your head on the bidet. It should probably have been stitched but we didn't realise that at the time. The long scar on your shin you got when you came running down the stairs and straight into dad's old metal tool box – I blame dad of course for leaving it in the middle of the room and for having such a stupid old dangerous thing in the first place. I think you were about seven then. It took ten stitches and you were very brave. Aged nine, you bit your tongue so badly that you couldn't eat solids for a whole week! You had been running around during break time at school and collided with another boy at full speed. I assume you were also talking or laughing at the time and that's how you bit your tongue. When the school nurse rang and asked me to collect you because you had bitten your tongue, I told her that I didn't think biting one's tongue was serious enough to miss half a day of school. She then assured me that it was quite serious and when I actually saw you, I had a real shock, especially as you could barely talk because your mouth was full of ice cubes. Your tongue was about an inch thick and totally blue – it was scary. It took a good two weeks to get back to normal during which time you stayed at school only half days as you could not eat normal food – I had to puree all the vegetables for you and feed you soups and smoothies.

You always did really well at school and won quite a few prizes. In your last year at pre-prep, you even won a special Christmas Carol competition! Do you remember?

The whole school had to sing it as the final song in the Carol concert! And then of course you got the Leaver's Maths prize which was no big surprise really – I would have been shocked if you hadn't. Your form teacher once said that if ever you had a different result to hers in a maths problem, she would immediately check her answer as it was more likely that she made a mistake than you! Not to forget all the form prizes which you got every term! So just be careful when you start throwing out some of the books – check the first page – as they might have been given to you as a form prize. Apart from excelling academically, you were also very popular with your peers because you were extremely sociable. At pre-prep there was hardly a day when you didn't either have friends round or went home with somebody. Once you started prep, this changed slightly as you often played sport after school as well as having a lot more homework, so socialising had to be limited to Fridays and weekends. Once you transferred to the scholarship class it got slightly more serious, more for us than you, because you were thinking of refusing your place with the argument that you didn't just want to work hard and have no fun so we had to promise that we would not make you miss any party or social event because of homework or exams (we lied of course – which parent wouldn't?!). You finally agreed to try it but with the option of dropping out if you hated it. Well, you stuck with it and got your scholarship in the end! And you were the only boy in the scholarship class who managed to play in all three 'A' teams – rugby, football and cricket – for the entire two years! And due to thirteen top grade GCSEs followed by five top A levels you also got a senior scholarship – throughout which you still continued with all your sport and, apart from when you were injured, never missed a training session in all these years! Forgive me, I know you remember all this anyway but I always felt that you just never realised how impressive a record this is. You always brushed it aside as if it were nothing special. Let me tell you, it is very special and something you can always be proud of! I know you will continue to do well and Goodness knows what might be if ever you worked really hard! But all work and no fun – that's not you, is it? You want to have a good time as well. That's fine most of the time and obviously hasn't hindered you much academically but there will be occasions in life when your effort and ambition has to take priority. Remember, competition is fierce and for every job and position, there's a multitude of candidates.

Try and keep up playing the guitar – you are quite good at it and you enjoy it which is the most important thing. Piano, I agree was not your forte and you were right to give it up after grade 3. I was a bit upset at the time but realised that there was no point in forcing you, especially after I'd received a phone call from your piano teacher at school asking why you hadn't turned up for the last three lessons! I can't believe that you'd actually thought you'd get away with it! When I asked you that evening how your piano lesson went, you said it was good and your teacher was happy with your progress. It was the first time (and one of the very few, I think) you lied to me and you clearly weren't practised in it because it was all too obvious – even if I hadn't known the truth, I would have been suspicious because of your body language. So when I asked you again, you replied first that you'd forgotten but eventually owned up that you didn't want to carry on with piano but you'd really like to start drums and had already spoken to the drum teacher at school who could fit you in next term. We made you pay for one of the missed piano lessons but you did start drum kit lessons and, much to our surprise, carried on up to grade 6 which you even passed with a merit! It seems it was the right choice! To us, it proved various things about you – strong will, determination and good judgement. The latter was probably the one that surprised and pleased us the most. The others were apparent from the day you were born! Unfortunately for you though, I too was very strong willed. And whilst I gave in and indulged you many times, there were certain things that were too important to let you have your way and I still believe that it was my duty to be firm on occasions as I'm convinced that children need discipline, set limits and routine. At the same time, and luckily for you, I'm also an ardent believer that childhood should be filled with lots of fun. Dad fully agreed with me on most of this – it was the fun element where I needed to convince him at times. He always moaned when I arranged these epic birthday parties for you, like hiring a coach and taking you and your friends out all day to a farm or go-carting, or paintballing or quad biking – always the whole class plus friends from nursery we had stayed in touch with, plus boys from other classes you were friendly with, so about 30–40 in all, but despite the initial objections, dad was always present and supportive on the day and it was so rewarding to see you all having so much fun. We also often had a house full of kids, and then dad did make sure he wouldn't come home until they had all left and everything was peaceful and quiet.

You always had a natural tendency to eat healthily. It started when you were a toddler. You needed lots of water but you hated fizzy drinks, even fizzy water. So I had to make sure I carried a bottle of still water around for you. And your stomach would not tolerate chocolate (I was so pleased) and every time you had some, you'd throw up – once into my handbag! We think it was caused by once, when you were very little, eating too much chocolate which you'd managed to get hold of at a birthday party when we weren't looking. So until about four, you preferred fruit to anything sweet! Sadly, once this phase passed, you made up for lost time. But you still liked healthy food, always loved fruit, vegetables and salads. Often after you'd been out with friends, other mothers would ask me in amazement how I managed to make you eat salads! Well, it was simple – you liked them! I think you were about ten when you had your first MacChicken – not with us, I hasten do add, and you really didn't like them at first. This changed of course. In the same way that you started to love Coke and I refused to have any in the house and you were only allowed it when we went to a restaurant. Well, I guess it didn't matter as long as you ate healthily at meal times. I know you eat well now and are quite health conscious (and I hope you never stop), I'm sure being sporty has a lot to do with it. I also know you still love chocolate and that's fine, just make sure you look after your teeth – keep brushing them regularly even when you have a late night and all you want to do is fall into bed

– it only takes two minutes but the reward lasts a lifetime! And make sure you visit the dentist at least once, preferably twice, a year – it is money well spent, trust me!

Dad just said this is turning into the same rigmarole as when you were four years old and I wrote the first 'Just in Case …' as dad and I were supposed to go away for the weekend, leaving you with Erika, the sweetest and best au pair we ever had. I got so upset and cried so much whilst writing the note that we decided not to go away in the end! Silly, isn't it? If it was meant to be, something could have happened to us when going out just for an evening. Anyway, Dad says that this time he will not cancel our trip!

You always wanted a dog but we always thought it was too much effort, taking it for a walk, needing someone to look after it during holidays etc. So to compensate, we got fish, rabbits, cats and a turtle – it would have been so much easier to just give in and get a dog! Think about that should you ever find yourself in a similar dilemma. Oh, and I almost forgot all the grasshoppers and crickets, we even brought them back from Germany and Austria! At one point we had about twenty five which you kept in a large transparent plastic box and fed them with grass, leaves and fresh water. The amazing thing is that several actually survived captivity for a few weeks. Sadly there were casualties and we eventually released the final "Magnificent Seven" as we called them in Hyde Park. Oh, and there was another involuntary 'pet' – remember the toad you held captive for a few days inside your sandpit until it somehow managed to escape despite you jamming the lid on it?

You were always a great enthusiast and when you liked

something, you did so with heart and soul. For your fourth birthday, one of your friends gave you a batman outfit – you wore it day and night! I had to get you a second one so that it could be washed in between. You grew very attached to certain things. Do you remember that big, old teddy bear you used to have? Your uncle gave you that when you were still a baby because you had taken an instant shine to it the moment you saw it at their house. It had belonged to your older cousin so was neither new nor particularly good quality in the first place, but it was massive, a head taller than you at the time and took up half your cot (there are some pictures of it somewhere). The many times I tried to get rid of it! Even after you stopped sleeping with it, it had to remain in your room seated on the chair in the corner. I think you were about twelve when I was allowed to put it away, not throw it away, you never gave me permission for that although I eventually did of course but I don't think it's that long ago!

Until you were about seven, you never went to sleep without one of us reading you a bedtime story, even when you were already reading your own books. Your first favourite book was "The Lost Sheep" – which we had to read at least once, sometimes twice, an evening. It was an interactive book and you enjoyed lifting up the flaps to uncover the pictures underneath and finally find the sheep even though you knew very well what you'd find under each flap! Other favourites were 'The Hungry Caterpillar', 'Where the Wild Things Are' and, of course, 'The Nu Nu Tree' which you bought yourself, aged five, during school book week. There were many more but those are the ones I most remember.

Once you could walk, at ten months, I enrolled you in a baby gym called 'Mini Muscles'. The sessions were held at the Budokwai Club and we attended twice a week – it was like an exercise class for toddlers ranging from walking stage to eighteen months and you would do forward rolls, run from one end of the hall to the other, climb some gym equipment, walk across a narrow beam whilst holding my hand etc. The next step up from that was 'Crechendo' – similar thing but a little more demanding regarding the exercises – which you attended weekly from eighteen months until you started nursery.

As you know, I'm very keen on hygiene, always have been, so naturally when you were born I kept sterilising everything you might come in contact with and once you started bottle feeding, I was already fully equipped with two electric sterilisers – one for home and one for travelling! You were about six or seven months old, so still crawling rather than walking, when we were spending the weekend with friends and their two dogs, one a puppy, in the country. You know of course what's coming and I'm aware that you have heard the story many times before but, lest you should forget, here is another reminder. As mentioned before, you adored dogs and this new puppy was just about your size and very similar in temperament to you – playful and into everything! It was obvious from the moment we arrived there that you were very fond of each other and that we had to keep a watchful eye on you. Apart from the fact that puppies have very sharp little teeth, a home with two dogs seriously lacks hygiene. So we spent the first few hours crawling on the floor with you and 'Buster' and wiping your hands and mouth every five minutes and only relaxed once you were asleep. I mentioned before that you were not a delicate looking baby and your strong, chubby legs, together with several months practice, had turned you into a crawling 'Speedy Gonzalez' and it is that I attributed your unnoticed escape to the next morning. It could only have been a split second during which you must have zoomed out of the bedroom door and when we had caught up with you, we found you in the kitchen with the puppy, on his blanket, sharing his bone – literally chewing on one end whilst he gnawed on the other! I was horrified and it took me a while before I could see the funny side of it. I threw away the sterilisers after that.

All our worldly goods are of course yours – chuck out what you don't want but be careful that you don't get rid of something too hastily when you might be able to sell it – we don't have hugely valuable stuff but a lot of our things are very good quality and definitely saleable. Hang on to the paintings and the antiques as they might increase in value. As for the jewellery, there are some very nice pieces which I'm sure my future daughter in law will appreciate and I would love to think that some of the rings will one day be worn by my grand daughter or your daughter in law! I'm not really worried about these things, I just want to make sure, well, as far as I can, that you don't have financial problems … like we had. I'm so sorry that we could never give you all the things you longed for and which we so wanted you to have but I do hope your memory won't focus on the shortcomings but reflect on the positive side of our parenting (I'm sure there was one!). There's plenty of photographic evidence that your childhood was happy! Tons of photo albums (one of my obsessions) and DVDs, and I urge you to look at them from time to time – it might be difficult at first but I promise, it will get easier (time heals all wounds and all that rubbish – but it's true). Discard all the loose pictures in the red box – they are mainly duplicates of those in the albums or weren't good enough to make the album in the first place – and there are just too many of them. Be a bit more ruthless than me. I'm such a hoarder, I hope you haven't inherited that from me. Dad of course is the other extreme – if it was up to him, we'd have a few framed pictures on the mantle piece and that would be it! So, try and find a happy medium – that, in my opinion, is the key to everything in life – balance! I don't like extremes. Manic-depressives epitomise extremes for me.

Obviously, you will have to make some arrangements for the cat before you leave for uni – Auntie Mary might help, if you ask nicely (beg, if you have to). I'm so sorry we won't be able to see you off. But I know you will be fine! You have always had this ability to rise above and you will need to do this now. You have such a promising future ahead of you and I know you will take every opportunity to continue to make us proud but most of all to do justice to your abilities. You are about to take up your rightful place at the best university in the world and this is just the beginning of your very successful and bright future.

When you are ready, maybe once you've finished uni, sell the house and buy a flat in town, near work preferably. Don't do anything too hasty though, check out the market first and remember – it's location, location, location! The better the location, the safer you'll be, plus the property is more likely to keep its value during a recession. But all that has time. The most important thing to concentrate on right now is your studies. I know you will enjoy university life – live it to the full (by that I mean: embrace the fun as well as studying!) and treasure every moment of it because it is over far too quickly.

I'm so sorry you have to read this now. So soon. I had always hoped that we'd be around during your university years, when you get your first job, maybe see you married. I would have liked to be here long enough for you to be pleased to get rid of us! Be around until I finally felt I could let go, but now? Well, ready or not, we have no say in it and as you read this, you too have no choice but to accept what happened and carry on without us. Life is cruel and right now it seems at its cruellest! Yet, we've also been very lucky and have a lot to be grateful for – you are eighteen, almost an adult! Imagine, if you would have had to read one of my earlier letters, say, a few years ago – shorter letter, but the situation so much more tragic! Now at least you don't need a legal guardian and you are off to uni where, during term time, you will learn to fend for yourself and you'll be so busy that you won't miss us. Make sure you stay with family at Christmas, not with friends and their family (unless they are Jewish, Muslims or Buddhists), it would be too upsetting, and please do not stay at home on your own! The first year will be the worst, it will get easier eventually.

There's so much more … but dad's getting quite impatient. So, my love, in the hope that I shall have to write many more 'Just in Case' notes before you actually have to read one, here is a final reminder: We love you, and I hope that one day you too will experience such happiness as you have given us.

Leaving the pages scattered on the table in front of him, not bothered about wiping away his tears, he lies down on the sofa, still unable to believe they are gone … not to see them ever again. It seems so unreal … even after the funeral.